LURE OF
obsession

LURE OF
obsession

Book #1 of the Muse Chronicles

LISA KESSLER

Lure of Obsession Copyright © 2016 by Lisa Kessler
Print Edition

All rights reserved, including the right to reproduce, distribute, or transmit in any form or by any means. For information regarding subsidiary rights, please contact the Author.

This book is a work of fiction. Names, characters, places, and incidents are the product of the author's imagination or are used fictitiously. Any resemblance to actual events, locales, or persons, living or dead, is coincidental.

Visit Lisa's website: Lisa-Kessler.com
Sign up for Lisa's newsletter: goo.gl/qaIIiS

Edited by Double Vision Editorial, Danielle Poiesz
Cover design by Fiona Jayde Media
Interior Design by BB eBooks
Vase Icon made by Freepik from www.flaticon.com is licensed under CC BY 3.0

Manufactured in the United States of America First Edition August 2016

ISBN: 978-0-9976274-2-8

Other Novels by Lisa Kessler

The Muse Chronicles
LURE OF OBSESSION
LEGEND OF LOVE

The Night Series
NIGHT WALKER
NIGHT THIEF
NIGHT DEMON
NIGHT ANGEL
NIGHT CHILD

The Moon Series
MOONLIGHT
HUNTER'S MOON
BLOOD MOON
HARVEST MOON
ICE MOON
BLUE MOON

Stand Alone Works
BEG ME TO SLAY
FORGOTTEN TREASURES
ACROSS THE VEIL

Dedication

This one is for my stepmom, Vivian, who has spent most of her life as a teacher inspiring the next generation to reach for their dreams.

Thanks for always loving me and my kids like your own.

CHAPTER 1

MEL STEPPED OUT of her car and froze. Damn. The condo was dark. Pitch dark. Nia never turned off a light, let alone all of them. Ever.

Worst-case scenarios played across her mind until she wanted to jump back in her car and drive away. Mel rubbed her hand up her arm, quelling the goose bumps rising on her skin. She forced herself to try to be optimistic. Maybe Nia went out earlier in the afternoon and, by some freak chance, didn't leave any lights on?

No way. That was horseshit, and Mel knew it. She'd lived with Nia for two years now. The girl was incapable of facing the dark.

Mel took a deep breath. Coming up with positive scenarios was difficult for her. The day she turned eighteen, the Muse of Tragic Poetry blossomed inside her, and with it came a penchant for tragedy. The glass was not only half-empty in her mind, but it could shatter at any moment. The awakening of her muse also caused her to have crazy dreams about a run-down theater and a group of women like her, who had a higher calling.

Now, ten years later, she'd found her soul sisters,

her fellow muses. Although they were mortal women only embodying the original Greek muses, each of her sisters had been chosen as a vessel—for reasons that were only clear to the gods themselves—to inspire the next generation of mankind. Together they'd worked and saved and pooled their money to buy the theater before it was marked for demolition, and together, they would restore it. The Theater of the Muses, *Les Neufs Soeurs,* would once again bring together the thinkers and artists and dreamers of the world.

But in spite of the progress toward their ultimate goal, she still struggled against a part of herself that continued to live in a perpetual state of angst.

Standing in the dark street where she could be hit by a car or abducted by an ax murderer wasn't helping.

Before she slammed the car door, she leaned in, snagging her messenger bag from the passenger seat. Her students' English papers still needed grading. *This is probably nothing.*

With the bag slung over her shoulder, she locked the car and crossed to her front door.

Even the porch light, Nia's twenty-four hour beacon, was off. A chill slithered down Mel's spine like a viper. Her roommate, the reborn Muse of Astronomy, didn't have energy conservation on her radar. She was all about stars and beacons of light in the darkness.

Talons of dread sank into the muscles on Mel's shoulders, and her chest constricted. The silence magnified each click as she slid her key into the lock.

She opened the door slowly, her hand searching for the switch on the wall beside the door.

Light flooded the room, and her heart stopped. Nia's lifeless blue eyes gazed up from the floor at the base of the stairs.

"No!" Mel collapsed next to her, pressing her fingers against Nia's neck in search of a pulse. No sign of a heartbeat but her skin was still warm. Her head was at an impossible angle, a small halo of blood framing her blond hair like a shadow.

"No," she breathed. "Nia, no." Mel blinked back hot tears, turning toward the staircase and looking it up and down. What had happened? Had she fallen?

With a trembling hand, Mel reached over to close Nia's eyes. Then she scrambled back, her stomach twisting. While her mind was always quick to envision the worst, this was the first time reality had lived up to her expectations—maybe even beyond. She made it back outside to the porch before she lost her dinner over the railing. Coughing, she fumbled for her cell phone in the pocket of her blazer and then dialed.

"9-1-1 what's your emergency?" the voice on the other end of the line asked.

"My roommate. She's—" Her voice cracked on a sob.

"Is she injured?"

"Yes. No. I mean, she was." Mel squeezed her eyes shut, begging her brain to engage. "She's dead. I think she fell. I don't know. I just got home."

The operator managed to coax her address from her and kept her on the line until the first police car pulled up, lights flashing. She wasn't sure how many others followed.

Mel was vaguely aware of the officers jogging toward her and then disappearing inside while she sat on the steps, lost in a fog of shock, oblivious to the cops and medics going in and out of her condo. But one thought gnawed at her, refusing to be ignored: the lights had been *off*.

Nia wouldn't have come down the stairs in the dark. Not in a million years. The Muse inside of her thirsted for light. She didn't even *sleep* in the dark. So who had turned them off?

"Are you Melanie Jacoby?"

She flinched at the sound of the stranger's deep voice and blinked to find herself staring up at a broad-shouldered man dressed in navy-blue slacks and a white dress shirt. His cuffs were rolled up, exposing chiseled forearms. A tie hung loosely around his neck, the top button unfastened.

"Mel," she muttered, lifting her gaze to his face. He had a strong jawline and bright green eyes, almost gray, in stark contrast to his dark hair. "Call me Mel."

"I'm Detective Malone." He paused, giving me a second to keep up through the fog of shock. "I need to ask you a few questions."

"Am I a suspect?" she blurted out.

He cocked a brow and pulled a small spiral notepad

from his pocket. "Should you be?"

Under different circumstances, she might have found this guy attractive, but right now, her inner muse had her too wired with tragic twists to focus on much else. Wasn't it enough that her roommate was dead? Couldn't that be enough tragedy for one night?

"No." She sighed. "I wasn't here when this happened, so I don't think I'll be much help with your questions. None of this makes sense."

He studied her for a moment and then slipped his pen back into his pocket. "We can do this later." Detective Malone walked past her to the door and stopped. "Do you have family nearby? Anyone I can call for you?"

"My sisters. Well, not really. Friends, I guess. Like sisters." She shut her mouth, saving herself from more incomplete sentences.

He mumbled something to another officer about the medical examiner signing off on something, but she couldn't make out his words. A black van pulled up, and her vision blurred with another wave of tears. They were coming for Nia. No, *not* for Nia.

For the *body*.

Detective Malone came around in front of her, blocking the view of the medical examiner's vehicle and its occupants while they unloaded a gurney.

She wiped her eyes and looked up at him. "Am I free to go?"

He held out a travel-sized pack of Kleenex. "I'm not

sure you should be driving. Why don't you come with me to the station? We can talk, and I'll treat you to a bad cup of coffee."

"You make it sound pretty tempting." She tugged out a tissue and stood up while she returned the almost-empty pack. She wiped her eyes and nose, and the tissue filled her lungs with his masculine scent, a combination of the ocean and something else that pulled at her. She couldn't put her finger on it.

But for a split second, it almost made her forget…

Mel focused on his face instead of on the people with the latex gloves who were passing behind him. "Make it Starbucks and you're on."

The corner of his mouth quirked, hinting at a smile that might make her knees weak if her friend wasn't lying lifeless a few feet away.

"You got it." He tipped his head toward the street. "Let's get out of here and let them finish up."

He grabbed the arm of another plainclothes officer, talking to him in low tones. They both glanced her way. Subtlety didn't seem to be a priority at the moment. Detective Malone returned to her. "My partner will stay and gather evidence. Let's see if we can find you some coffee."

She followed him to his car and got in. Through the window, an officer roped off the stairs to her front door with yellow crime-scene tape. Mel gnawed at her lower lip, fighting to keep it together. As Detective Malone pulled away from the curb, she closed her eyes and wished this nightmare were just a dream.

HE WATCHED THEM drive away before stuffing his black leather gloves into the backpack. His hands still trembled with adrenaline.

His first kill.

Murder hadn't been as difficult as he'd imagined. The Muse of Astronomy had been wearing her iPod, humming on her way out of the bedroom with running shoes in hand. He'd been waiting in the spare room, blade at the ready, but when she'd passed him on her way to the staircase, he'd recognized his chance. One firm shove and gravity had done the dirty work for him.

She'd cried out once before her head struck the stairs, snapping her neck. He wondered if she'd seen his masked face before her world went dark. He hoped so.

Urania—the first muse to cross off the Order's target list.

Of course, he'd hoped to finish both muses tonight. He'd been waiting in the kitchen, expecting her roommate to rush to the phone. Instead, she had surprised him by running out front and vomiting. She'd made her 911 call from the porch on her cell, and he'd been forced to slip out the back before the police arrived.

No matter. He would find her again soon enough.

Once the golden mask of Kronos was tucked safely inside his pack, he hooked it over his shoulder and walked away from the condominium complex.

The Order of the Titans was a step closer to victory.

And the glory rested squarely on *his* shoulders.

DETECTIVE NATE MALONE watched Mel pick at the cardboard sleeve of her latte cup. Under the blue fluorescent lights of the police station, her pale skin revealed a light dusting of tiny freckles along her nose and cheeks. He didn't mean to notice them, but it was too late now. He also didn't mean to notice her deep-brown eyes that opened the window to an old soul.

He caught himself wanting to see her smile. What would her laughter sound like?

Shit. What was wrong with him? He'd sat across the table from witnesses hundreds of times and he'd never felt so…drawn in. He shifted in his chair, struggling to stay focused on his purpose in bringing her here.

To protect her.

The thought jarred him further. He popped his ballpoint pen. "I need to ask you a few questions about your roommate." She nodded but didn't make any eye contact. "Was she depressed? Any mention of wanting to hurt herself?"

Her eyes met his, a brief flash of anger sparking in

them. "This wasn't a suicide. Nia had big plans."

"Good to know." He didn't miss the fire in her stare. In spite of the evidence pointing to an accident, she was still convinced someone hurt her friend. He jotted a note and set his pen down. "Can you trace your steps for me from this afternoon until you found her?"

She sipped her latte. "I teach poetry and classic literature at Crystal City High. I finished my last class, survived another staff meeting about the importance of standardized test scores, and then I gathered my students' papers and left."

"Did you make any stops on your way home?"

She nodded, fiddling with the sleeve on her latte again. "I got gas and stopped at Bartlett's for a cup of soup. Nia was heading to the theater tonight. I thought I'd be on my own for dinner."

There was no logical excuse for the surge of desire to comfort her, but recognizing that it was irrational didn't lessen its power. What the hell was wrong with him? *Keep it professional, Malone.*

"What theater is this? Did she work there?" His pen was poised over his notepad, waiting for her to answer.

After a beat, she said, "We own it. When we finish, it's going to be a recreation of The Theater of the Muses in Paris. My sisters and I bought it last summer. It still looks pretty crappy, but we're fixing it up."

He raised a brow. "So you and your roommate were related?"

She sipped her drink and shrugged. He tried not to watch her wet her lips with her tongue. "Not blood related, but we're all close, like sisters."

Nate rubbed at the back of his left shoulder, over the birthmark shaped like a half moon. It had never bugged him before, but now it was staring to itch like a son of a bitch, and his skin was hot all of a sudden. Pushing up his shirtsleeves, he continued his interview; taking notes until he felt sure the crime scene techs would be finished at Mel's place.

"That's enough for now," he said after ten more minutes of questions. "Is there a friend or family you can stay with tonight?"

"I'll call my friend Callie when I get home." She rubbed her temples. "You still think it was an accident, don't you?"

He closed his notepad, tucking it into his pants pocket. "There were no signs of a forced entry. I didn't see any defensive wounds, either. The medical examiner is leaning toward an accident unless we find something to the contrary…"

"But there were no lights on." Her dark eyes met his, pleading. "Not even the porch light. I know it sounds crazy, but it was *always* on. Nia was all about light. She never turned them off."

He got up, crossing to her side of the table. "Maybe it burned out. I'll check it out when we get back to your place."

"Thanks."

She didn't look convinced, but what could he do? All the evidence pointed to an accident. No one broke in, and judging by the interview with Mel, her roommate hadn't been depressed. But none of those facts changed the outcome.

Her friend was still dead.

He led her back to the parking lot and into his unmarked sedan. The dispatch radio provided background noise to cover the heavy silence as he drove. Every time he glanced over at his passenger, her attention was focused out the window. Most likely she was lost in thought and shocked that life could end so suddenly, or maybe she was wondering how she'd make the rent without her roommate.

As a detective, he'd witnessed many stages of grief, but something about this woman got under his skin. Seeing her in pain had him wanting to get involved, to help her. It made the case feel personal. Not good.

He parked at the curb and guided her up the walkway and under the police tape. She unlocked the door, and Nate stepped into the thick darkness first. Running his hand along the wall, his fingers brushed a switch.

An image flashed in his mind—a large gloved hand touching the switch—before the porch light blazed to life, blinding him for a moment. He flinched at the image before he could stop himself. What the hell? He rubbed his eyes, blinking.

Maybe he imagined it. But it sure looked like a man's hand turning off the porch light.

"It wasn't burned out," Mel said softly, taking a step back. "Someone turned it off. I told you. Someone else was here."

"The accident happened during the day. She may have accidentally bumped the switch and turned it off."

Mel shook her head, rushing between the light switches, turning them all on until the shadows were banished from the downstairs living area and hallway. She looked up at him, fear lining her eyes.

"She didn't 'bump' them all. Someone did this."

"I'll stay with you while you get your things and call your friend." Nate fought the urge to pull her into his arms. Seeing her frightened agitated him, which made no sense because most people he came in contact with were scared.

"Callie." She nodded with a dazed look as she stepped over the numbered markers on the floor where her friend's body had landed. "I've got to call Callie. She needs to know what happened to Nia."

She wandered up the stairs, mumbling and turning on more light switches as she went. Once she disappeared down the hallway, he narrowed his eyes, searching for any piece of evidence they might have missed, any sign that another person had been in the condo.

But nothing looked out of place, no overturned plants, no phone knocked to the floor. Nothing. Mel's roommate had a tragic, accidental fall. There was nothing pointing to foul play. But maybe he could come back and dust the other light switches for fingerprints.

He blew out his frustrations and leaned against the banister.

Another image appeared in his mind. The victim falling, the terror in her eyes before her head struck a stair and then another. Standing behind her, at the top of the staircase was a man dressed in a black hooded robe, wearing a gold mask.

"What the hell?" Nate jumped away from the railing and rubbed his face, a cold sweat covering his back. He was probably just overtired and concerned about his witness—about Mel.

She appeared at the top of the stairs with a duffel bag. "Are you all right?"

In that moment, staring up at her, he realized something had awakened inside him like a sixth sense. "No." He shook his head. "No, I'm far from it."

Frowning, she came down to his side. "What is it?"

"Just a cop's hunch." How could he put what had just happened into words without sounding completely insane? Though, maybe he was insane. "Let's get you to your friend's place."

He rushed her out of the condo; adrenaline pumping until he thought his heart might burst. Something was very wrong.

CHAPTER 2

NATE GRIPPED THE wheel so tight, he feared he might yank it right off the steering column. Mel sat beside him, still in a daze. At least it distracted her from noticing how close he was to losing it.

What the hell had happened back at her place? It had to be an overactive imagination. But he'd never had one before, and why would he have imagined that gold mask? He'd never seen one like it, so why would he dream it up?

He had too many questions and not nearly enough answers.

"Make a right here," Mel said, pointing down a dimly lit side street.

Crystal City wasn't huge like Los Angeles, which was a couple of hours south, but with a population nearing 300,000 people, there were still streets he'd never explored. Callie's was one of them.

"Lothlórien Lane?" He could almost hear the mental file cabinet rolling open in his mind, while he searched for why he recognized the name.

"Cal is a huge Tolkien fan."

"Ah, right. The Lord of the Rings." He nodded.

"That's where I heard it before."

"Yeah, the elves lived there or something. When she found this street, she moved here as soon as a house came on the market."

Unusual house-hunting technique, but he wasn't one to judge. He still didn't own a home—not that he couldn't afford it, but the commitment... Well, commitment was...not his scene. Not anymore. It was too final.

The road ended in a cul-de-sac. He rounded it slowly when the floodlights came on in front of a modest single-level home with stone trim. A woman in sweats came out as he pulled to the curb and parked.

"Is that Callie?" he asked.

Opening her door, Mel nodded. "Yeah." She hurried out of the car and over to embrace her friend.

He tried to give them some privacy while Mel broke the bad news. He moved slowly as he unloaded her bag from the trunk. He had just turned toward the house when Callie stepped into his path. Her cheeks were wet with tears as she held out her hand.

"I'm Callie O'Connor. And you are?"

He set the bag down and shook her hand. "Detective Malone."

She had short, black hair, dark-brown eyes, and a pert nose that reminded him of a pixie. Maybe Mel's mention of elves was influencing his perspective.

Callie stepped back and wiped her cheeks. "Thanks for being Mel's hero tonight."

"I wouldn't call giving her a ride over here *heroic*. I just wanted to be sure she's safe."

Mel walked over and picked up her bag. The breeze blew through her auburn hair and teased the bare skin of his forearm. She tucked a stray lock behind her ear. "Thanks for the lift."

He nodded, confused by the yearning to pull her into his arms. Nurturing and comforting weren't usually part of his repertoire. "I'm sorry about your friend."

"You'll catch whoever did this, right?" Callie asked.

His gaze shifted to the five-foot-nothing young woman. "We're working on figuring out exactly what happened."

Mel cleared her throat. "They think the lights were off and she fell."

She paused and Callie crossed her arms. Mel looked statuesque beside her petite friend. He estimated she might be five foot ten, but he was over six feet tall. She'd fit just right in his arms, he realized. He rubbed his eyes, wishing he could massage his brain back toward sanity.

"Oh she'd never turn out the lights, Detective." Callie widened her stance, her hip leaning out to the side. "She even kept night-lights plugged in, in every room but Mel's."

He bobbed his head. "I have that in my notes." The gold mask flashed through his mind. Could he ask them about it without sounding completely nuts? He paused for a beat but decided to go for it. "Do either of you know if she might have been involved in a cult, or maybe was aware of someone who might have been?"

Mel arched a brow. "A cult?" She glanced at Callie and then back to him. "I lived with her for two years and she hasn't met with anyone but us during that time."

"All right. It still appears to be an accidental fall, but just in case, keep your doors locked and your security system on."

Callie tipped her head, her fist coming to rest on her hip. "I've got a croquet mallet and I know how to use it. We'll be just fine."

He gave her a stern look. "A wooden club is no replacement for a system that'll send a black-and-white over to be sure you're fine."

She groaned. "Mel's freaked out enough without you making us paranoid."

His shoulders bunched up. "I'm trying to keep her safe."

"If you're so sure it was an accident, then why would we be in any danger?"

That was the million-dollar question he had no desire to answer yet. "I'd better get out of here so you can rest. I'll be in touch, Mel." He handed both women his card. "My cell number is at the bottom if you need me."

HIS TAILLIGHTS VANISHED around the corner, and Mel glanced at Callie. "He knows something he's not sharing. Why would a cult have anything to with this?"

Callie shrugged. "I don't know. But after talking to both of us, if he still believes Nia was walking around in the dark, then he's not much of a detective."

"In his defense, he's probably never met a woman with a Muse reborn inside of her. Nia was addicted to light…a bright star." Her voice wavered. She swallowed a sob before it could escape. "We should get inside."

Once they were safely in the house, Callie set the dead bolt and then went to the kitchen to pour two glasses of iced tea. "Any idea who would want to hurt Nia?"

Mel took a sip, doing her best to bottle up her emotions. "No. Other than us and her coworkers in the light-fixtures department at Home Depot, she never spent time with anyone."

"Do you have her mom's number?"

Mel cringed. She'd been so lost in her own shock and pain, she hadn't even thought about Nia's family. They had no idea what had happened. Before the Muse of Astronomy awoke inside of her, Nia had simply been a daughter and an older sister. Now she was gone.

"Mel?" Callie's voice took on that calming professional tone she used with her psych patients on the military base. "We should call them before the coroner does. We knew her."

Mel swiped at the tear weaving its way down her face. Callie was right. But the thought of hearing Nia's parents cry... The Muse of Tragic Poetry inside of her soul loved tragedies in movies and books, but no matter how hard she wished it, this wasn't fiction.

She pulled out her cell phone and stared at it. "I can't do it."

Callie took the phone from her and scrolled through the contacts. "They're in Texas, right? I hope I can catch them before they're in bed."

Mel stared out the window. There was no convenient time to learn that your daughter was dead. No polite hour existed for that kind of call.

While Callie spoke in soft, empathetic tones behind her, Mel kept replaying the night's events in her head, trying to recall every detail of the crime scene. Had she missed something? Had anyone dashed out of the condo complex? Anything been out of place?

But other than the lights being out, nothing seemed off.

Then she turned her attention to Detective Malone. Something bothered her about him. He'd been all business when he questioned her at the police station, and he seemed certain Nia's fall had been an accident. Case closed. But everything had changed when they got back to her place.

He'd walked her up to her porch and offered to go

inside to make sure it was safe, but the moment he'd touched the light switch, something shifted. When the lights came on, he'd been rubbing his eyes, pale and shaken up. She'd been preoccupied while it was happening, but thinking back, his placating tone had vanished and he'd suddenly wanted her out of the condo. *A cop's hunch,* he'd called it.

So why the change of heart about the danger?

"Mel, I'm going to text our sisters and have them come over. We need to put our heads together, and this will save me from having to repeat the awful story over and over." Callie was the Muse of Epic Poetry, so if anyone could rally them to circle the wagons and fight back, it would be her.

Mel nodded. "Okay. Tell them to be careful."

All we need is to lose another sister to a car wreck.

Mel massaged her temples, wishing she could wipe the dark thoughts from her mind. Being the vessel for the Muse of Tragic Poetry was no picnic. Although she tried to think positively, she was a glass-half-empty kind of girl.

Within the hour, eight muses were sitting and standing around Callie's living room. Mel stood in the corner, watching as Callie greeted each of them. Trinity and Erica were the Muses of Music and Lyrics, respectively. Best friends and roommates, they almost always traveled together, and you could usually hear them coming.

Not tonight, though. Dread hung heavy tonight,

silencing the duo.

Beside them, Polly stood behind Tera and braided her long, chocolate-colored hair. It was surreal to see Tera so stoic and still. The Muse of Dance was always in motion.

But not tonight.

Polly finished the braid and crossed her arms. Although technically she was the Muse of Harmony and Hymns, she was also integral to their finances for the theater renovation. She came from a rich family, and her trust fund saved their precious theater from its date with demolition.

Thalia lingered near the door. No doubt the lack of smiles ate at the Muse of Comedy, but she made no move to lighten the mood. A testament to the urgency in Callie's voice on the phone. She may not have told them what happened, but the message had been clear: the news wasn't good.

Even Clio, the Muse of History, sat at the edge of her chair, no sign of a book in her hands. Usually she was happiest reliving the past, which made getting her to notice the present challenging at best.

Callie finished her quiet greetings and turned around, her gaze prodding Mel to speak. She'd been hoping Callie might do it for her, but as the Muse of Epic Poetry, Cal probably wasn't a great choice to break the news. She'd blow everything into some quest, a battle between good and evil.

Being realistic wasn't always Callie's strong suit.

Gradually, all their stares landed on Mel. She bit the inside of her cheek, struggling to find her voice.

Thalia beat her to it, asking, "Where's Nia?"

Mel took a slow breath as she glanced around the room at the friends who had become like sisters to her. "Nia is…" She swallowed hard. "Nia is dead."

A couple of gasps broke the silence as the air sucked out of the room.

"What?" Polly dropped her arms, a crease marring her brow. "How? What happened?"

Mel's vision blurred behind a wave of tears. "I came home after work tonight and she was at the bottom of the stairs. She…fell."

Their questions piled on top of one another until Mel raised her hands. "The police think it was an accident, but when I came home, there weren't any lights on. Not even on the porch outside."

Whispers filled the room. Mel forced herself to hold back her tears at least a little while longer. "I think someone pushed her. She never would have turned off all the lights. Someone had to have done that after she died."

"Were they maybe hoping to grab you in the dark?"

Polly's question sent a chill creeping down Mel's spine as she shrugged. "I don't think so. There was no one there when I found her and called 9-1-1."

At least not that she'd seen.

Callie came over and wrapped a supportive arm around her shoulder. "Mel doesn't think Nia had any enemies, but we should all be careful. And if you think of anything that could help the police figure out what happened, let Mel know so she can pass information on to the detective working on the case."

"But they think she fell, right?" Clio wrung her hands as her gaze wandered between Callie and Mel. "Why would they help us?"

"I think Detective Malone believes me," Mel said. "He didn't want me to stay at the condo tonight."

Callie raised her free hand toward the kitchen. "I have some hot water for tea on the stove. Let's go sit down and make a list of anyone who may have known Nia. It's a place to start anyway."

Mel watched them go. Could someone have been waiting for her, too? But why? The only connection between her and Nia were the spirits of the muses inside of them, and no one else could possibly know that. Could they?

But nothing from the condo had been stolen and Nia didn't have any enemies that she knew of... What other motive could there be to connect them?

She shook her head almost violently. Impossible. She was letting her tendency toward tragedy get the best of her.

She stared at the door. But if it was true and someone was hunting the muses, then they were all in danger.

"I'm calling it a night. You going home soon, Nate?"

He glanced away from his computer screen for a second. "Yeah, I'm almost done here."

John had been his partner long enough to see right through his bullshit. But unlike John, Nate had nothing to go home to. No wife and kids, not even a dog.

John tipped his head toward the list on the monitor. "You don't think it was an accident, do you?" He heaved a disgruntled sigh. "There's no evidence anyone else was in that condo, Malone."

Nate leaned back in his chair. "According to her roommate, our vic had a thing for leaving all the lights on. But everything was off. Even the porch."

"Could've been our guys."

Nate nodded and minimized the window. "Maybe downstairs, but every light upstairs was off, too. None of our team was up in the bedrooms."

"What're you thinkin'?"

That I'm completely losing my shit.

"Just a hunch," he said instead. "I think she might be on to something."

"It's a stretch without any sign of forced entry."

"Unless our vic didn't believe in locking her doors, either." He made a note to ask Mel later.

John pulled a chair over. "I'll stay and help you out."

"It's probably nothing." Nate shook his head. "Go home and kiss Beth and the kids for me."

John gripped the back of the chair without sitting. "You should get out of here, too."

He glanced up at his partner, who somehow managed to look sympathetic and suspicious all at the same time.

"This isn't about Maggie," Nate insisted. For the first time, it didn't hurt to say her name.

"You sure about that?"

I'm not sure of anything anymore.

"Yeah. Just covering all our bases before the coroner reports it as an accidental death."

John's silent, piercing stare brought many suspects to unexpected confessions, but Nate was no suspect and he had no intention of talking about what he'd seen in Mel's condo.

Finally, his partner broke eye contact and stepped back. "All right, then. Catch you in the morning."

"See you then."

Nate reopened the search window the second John vanished down the hallway. A digital wall of masks stared back at him. His finger rolled the mouse in a slow downward scroll.

"Okay, you bastard. Where are you?"

CHAPTER 3

MEL'S ALIBI HAD checked out. Nate loosened his tie and popped the top button on his shirt. She had been in a staff meeting until five thirty the night before. What surprised him was discovering that she had come into work *today*. Everyone dealt with the death of a friend differently, and the shock of finding the body might have left her aching for normalcy. It was hard to tell how any given person would react, but he hadn't expected her to be teaching.

Standing in the hallway outside her English classroom, he glanced at his watch. Ten minutes left until her lunch break. Rather than interrupt, he leaned against the lockers and pulled out his cell phone. A guitar chord sounded, distracting him from skimming his e-mail. He frowned and moved closer to the door. Mel taught freshman English, Creative Writing, and Poetry. So why was someone inside playing the blues?

Mel's voice came through the door. "Do you see how the rhythm and tone of the poem mirror the music? Who wants to try next? Cara, why don't you come on up?"

The guitar music picked up again and a girl's nerv-

He started to speak, but his mouth went dry. Hanging on the wall behind Mel's desk was a large black mask with purple trim and a deep frown. On a normal day, he might not have even noticed the thing, but since he'd touched the light switch and the bannister at Mel's place last night, he'd been on edge.

Until the vision of the man in the golden mask flashed in his head, he'd never really given them much thought, but now the eyeless, soulless, frowning face on her wall had dread tightening around his gut like a vise.

Mel turned, following his gaze. "That's the Tragedy Mask. It represents tragedy in theater." Her focus shifted back to him, capturing his full attention. "Sort of a mascot for my high school English classes."

"I'm going to get out of your way," Trinity interrupted, her guitar case in hand. "See you at the theater later?"

Mel nodded, giving her a short embrace. "Yeah, I'll be by after work."

After Trinity left, Nate struggled to keep his eyes off the mask on the wall. "I wasn't expecting to find you working today."

Mel leaned against the edge of her desk. "Sitting around crying at Callie's place isn't going to bring Nia back. And the kids were really excited about the poetry project today. I couldn't call in a sub. They'd probably send some fresh-out-of-college Algebra teacher who would make them watch *Good Will Hunting* or something…" She pressed her lips together. "Sorry. I'm not

ous voice spoke between the chords. "I tried hard not to see." *Dun-dun-dun-dun-dun.* "But his smile grabbed hold of me." *Dun-dun-dun-dun-dun.* "It may not be headline news." *Dun-dun-dun-dun-dun.* "But I've got a bad case of the high school blues."

The classroom erupted in applause, and Nate smiled. Mel wasn't just teaching an English class; she was inspiring another generation. These kids would remember her long after they left these halls. Sadly, not all teachers had that gift.

When the bell rang, a river of teens flowed past him, buzzing about writing more poems, and songs and lyrics. They actually *wanted* to write and create. Amazing. After the flood of students dried up, he stepped into the doorway and discovered Mel had company.

A curvy woman with shoulder-length black hair and porcelain skin looked up from her guitar case and glanced at Mel. "Looks like you've got a guest."

Mel stopped sliding binders into her bag and straightened up. "Detective Malone." She gestured to her friend with the guitar. "This is Trinity. Trin, this is the detective working Nia's case."

Trinity closed the guitar case and stretched out her hand. "Good to meet you."

He gave her a firm handshake. "Heard you playing the blues in here."

Trinity chuckled, tossing her hair back over her shoulder. "Thanks. It was Mel's idea."

feeling very optimistic at the moment."

He almost smiled. Her devotion to her students was admirable, regardless of her current state of mind. "I've got a couple questions about the case for you. Do you have time now, or should I come back later?"

Mel straightened to her full height. Usually that meant she'd be adjusting her gaze downward, but Detective Malone still had a few inches on her. "If you don't mind watching me eat my sandwich, I've got an hour."

"Works for me."

She brought a black Velcro lunch sack out of her desk and led him to a large round worktable at the back of the room. Once they were seated, she withdrew a sandwich, an apple, and a soda from her bag.

"Do you still think it was an accident?" She pulled out her apple and took a bite.

He ignored her question and set a few printouts of masks before her. "Do any of these look familiar?"

She looked down at the images and nodded. "These are all masks of Kronos." She took a closer look. "Yeah. Different time periods maybe, but that's definitely Kronos." She lifted her gaze to meet his. "What do these masks have to do with any of this?"

He shifted in his chair and pulled out a pen. "Kronos. He was a Greek god or something, right?"

"Actually, he was a Titan. Zeus imprisoned him in the center of the Earth." She set her apple down. Her appetite was nonexistent today anyway. The meal was more out of habit than hunger. "And this will help us catch Nia's killer how?"

"I'm not sure." His green eyes mesmerized her for a moment. "But I think you're right… It wasn't an accident."

Dark thoughts whizzed through her mind. Everything from Detective Malone slapping cuffs on her wrists, to him confessing he killed Nia and she was about to be next. Mel let her hands slip off the table into her lap. She flexed her fingers before clenching them into tight fists in an effort to release some of the anxiety that her worst-case scenarios were dredging up.

"What changed your mind?"

A muscle jumped in his cheek as his attention shifted to the pages of Kronos's likenesses, but he didn't answer her question.

She nudged one of them. "If it will help, I have a great Greek mythology book I could loan you."

He slumped back in his chair, bringing one hand up behind his neck. His shirt barely contained his bicep. She swallowed and forced her gaze elsewhere. This was no time to get distracted, regardless of how well built this detective might be.

"The book couldn't hurt at this point," he said.

"Great." Mel got up, relieved for an excuse to put a little distance between them. She needed to stay focused on figuring out what happened to Nia, not how good Nate Malone might look without that shirt. She crossed to the bookcase on the far wall, running an index finger along the spines of collections of Edgar Allen Poe, Mary Shelley, and Shakespeare. "Do you have any leads?"

"Not anything to convince the medical examiner it wasn't an accidental fall."

She slid a small jade-colored hardcover from the shelf and turned around. His eyes moved up to her face. Had he been staring at her ass? Suddenly she didn't feel so bad about ogling his biceps. She bit the inside of her cheek to keep from smiling.

Seriously? Smiling?

She must've been in some kind of shock.

Mustering up as much indifference as she could, she walked over and placed the book in front of him. "If there's no evidence, then why the sudden change of heart?"

He looked up at her, and the urge to touch him swelled. She crossed her arms, no longer confident she could trust her hands.

"You told me she never turned off the lights, and they were all off, even upstairs. Your alibi checked out, so if it wasn't you and she never turned them off, then who did?"

She tapped her fingernail on the printouts he'd brought. "Where does our pal Kronos play into all this?"

He slid all the pages back together and put them into the manila file folder. "Call it a hunch for now."

She raised a brow. "Another *hunch*? What aren't you telling me?"

"Look, when I have something concrete, you'll be the first one to know." He stood up, taking both the mythology book and the folder in one large hand. "Thanks for the information and the book."

He was hiding something from her. "You're welcome." He turned to go and her heart hammered in her chest. "Detective Malone?"

He stopped and glanced back. "You can call me Nate."

Nate. She filed that away for later. "I'll be finished here at three thirty. I was planning on grading a few papers at the café at the end of the block before I meet my sisters at the theater. If you come by, I could give you a crash course on Kronos and the Golden Age of Man."

The corner of his lips tugged up in a lopsided smile that awoke the butterflies in her stomach. "I can use all the help I can get," he said. "I'll see you there."

Her classroom door closed behind him, leaving her in the silence to replay the conversation. She didn't know his secret yet, but she was going to find out.

"WE MIGHT HAVE a problem."

Ted Belkin sighed and lifted his head.

Marion was leaning against the doorway. "I just got word from the building inspector's office that those women you wanted me to keep an eye on came in today for a new permit on that theater."

The damned theater. *Les Neufs Soeurs,* the Cult of the Muses.

His blood pressure shot up as he tightened his grip on the computer mouse. "Thank you, Marion."

She nodded and headed out of the room, closing the door behind her. Ted snatched the phone receiver from its cradle, punching his frustration into the keypad.

"Yes?" a man said on the other end of the line.

He lowered his voice, staring at the back of his office door. "I thought you took care of them."

"As I reported last night, I was only able to eradicate one target. Urania, the Muse of Astronomy, is no more."

Ted tipped his leather chair back, shifting his gaze to the ceiling. "That's not enough. They were at the permit office today."

"Panic isn't going to further our cause."

"I'm not panicking, you little pissant. I don't think you realize the importance of keeping that theater from opening."

He paused long enough for Ted to begin wondering if he'd hung up. "I'm well aware of what's at stake, sir."

"Then get the damned job done. And for god's sake, find a contact in the building department and see if we can stall their project in the meantime."

"I understand. For the good of mankind."

"Exactly."

Ted slammed the phone back down into its cradle and swiveled his chair to stare out the window. From his office on the sixth floor, he could see the expanse of the Pacific glittering before him. A few miles offshore, his oilrig continued cutting through the rock at the bottom of the ocean, carving through the layers of the Earth. He twisted the heavy gold ring around his finger. It had been in his family for generations, passed down to each eldest child along with the family mission of once again ushering in the Golden Age of Man.

His great-great-grandfather had been the first of their Order to make physical progress toward the ultimate goal: to free the powerful prisoners from the center of the Earth. In 1896, off the coast of Santa Barbara, his great-great-grandfather used well-drilling equipment attached to the pier. It had been a start. The Order had been involved in mining on land, as well, but cave-ins and environmental impact studies slowed them to a crawl.

But offshore oil drilling kept their progress hidden from the public eye. As long as the population needed oil, he had the money to continue their quest, cutting deeper toward the Earth's core.

None of his ancestors had lived to see the success of

their quest. He would be the first, because this time, he'd given the Order a valuable tip, an ace up his sleeve. While he'd attended college, he'd dated a woman with a gift for music. She'd dazzled him at first, but as he got to know her better, he learned she was plagued with strange dreams about ancient Greece and a dilapidated theater here on the West Coast.

Over time, they'd drifted apart, but after graduation, he'd followed her to Crystal City and discovered that, as crazy as it seemed, his ex-girlfriend was connected with eight more women sharing the same dream of a worn-down theater slated for demolition. And each woman excelled at a different skill set, just as his ex had with music.

And then suddenly he knew who these women were.

The nine Greek Muses, awakened again for this generation of man and meant to inspire mankind forward in the sciences and the arts. They'd been brought together through the shared dream of a theater that could change the world. They were now united, driven in their passion to reopen the Theater of the Muses. The same Masonic think tank that had existed in France in the eighteenth century and catered to the likes of Voltaire and Benjamin Franklin.

But the Order was too close to success now, too close to the center of the Earth, to the Titans. The last things he needed were solar cars and homes. For over a century, his family had perfected the technology to drill oil offshore, but without humanity's need for the black gold, his funding would dry up. Literally.

He'd called a meeting, and the Order of the Titans had agreed with his assessment. This generation, the Order would be successful where previous generations had failed, because this time they would steal mankind's inspiration. They would kill the muses for the greater good.

Ted smiled. The Golden Age of Man would return, and he would be immortalized as the man with the vision to see the quest to its finish.

For the good of mankind.

CHAPTER 4

NATE OPENED THE coffee shop door and spotted Mel sitting at a table in the corner. Her dark-red hair hung like a veil, hiding her face, but somehow that didn't matter. His senses honed in on her the second he walked in. He'd like to blame it on his highly developed observation abilities, but police training had nothing to do with his strange attraction to this woman.

As he approached, she glanced up from her papers. "I didn't think you'd show."

He frowned. "Did I do something to make you think I'd stand up a woman who offered me help?"

"No." Mel chuckled and gestured toward the other chair. "But if there's a dark side or a tragedy to be found, that's the first place my mind goes."

He sat across from her, and his blood pressure already seemed to be normalizing just being near her. "Can I ask you something?"

She set her red pen down. "Sure."

"How did you come up with mixing the blues and poetry?"

"This is going to help with Nia's case?"

He ran a hand down his face. *Way to be professional, Malone. Shit.* "Never mind."

"Tell you what…" She leaned a little closer. "You answer my personal question, and I'll answer yours. And if we're brave enough, we can do one more round. Sound fair?"

He cocked a brow. Was she daring him? "I guess that depends on how personal your question is."

She took a sip of her coffee and slowly set the mug back on the table. "What happened at my condo the other night? Something shook you up when we went back there."

Damn it. He didn't think she had noticed. He tapped his pen on the folder, scrambling for something to tell her besides seeing a wacko in a gold Kronos mask shoving her friend down the stairs.

"I can't explain it." It was the truth. "But even though there's no evidence to prove your friend was murdered, I believe you."

Her expression softened. "Thank you." She glanced at his folder. "So you think Kronos pushed Nia down the staircase?"

Yes. He shook his head. "No. But there have been a couple sightings of robed men in these gold masks." Okay, so that wasn't exactly true. So far he'd only seen one in his head, but he had to tell her something, and until he could figure out if he was crazy, the truth wasn't an option.

She raised a brow. "Really? I haven't heard anything on TV."

He cleared his throat. "I think it's your turn to answer my question."

A barely-there smile tugged at her lips, distracting him for a moment. "I think the blues and poetry are a perfect match. The music helps the kids find a rhythm for their emotions on the page. Plus, it helps my students share with one another in a safe environment. Sometimes knowing you're not alone in your feelings—especially your tragedies—can make all the difference."

And sometimes being alone is the only way to keep the tragedy boxed up, he thought.

He sat back in his chair, pondering the woman across the table. "You seem pretty together for someone who just lost her friend."

She stared at her coffee cup. "I'm a lot of things, but *together* isn't one of them." She lifted her eyes. "I'll never sleep in that condo again. I'm staying at Callie's for now. I called the landlord to terminate the lease." She blinked back tears and shifted in her chair. "I'm pretty sure it's my turn to ask a question." Clearing her throat, she charged forward. "Have you ever been shot?"

He was going to get whiplash from her sudden changes in subject, but he chuckled. He couldn't help it. "Yeah."

When had tonight become a chance to get to know each other? He had a case to solve. But something about Mel made it tough for him to think straight.

"Twice," he went on. "A bullet grazed my right arm once, and I was hit in my vest another time. It cracked a rib, but I lived, so I count that as a win."

Mel sipped her coffee. "So what do you want to know about Kronos?"

He raised a brow at another abrupt change in the conversation. "Are you disappointed I couldn't dodge a couple bullets?"

A real smile teased her lips as she lowered her coffee mug. "On the contrary, I'm a sucker for a guy with scars, so for your protection, we should probably stick to the case."

"I'm not scared." Blood was suddenly pumping away from his brain, and for a split second, he considered taking off his shirt to show her his scar. He was losing his mind. Fast. "But I do have a case to work."

She nodded slowly. "Definitely for the best."

He didn't agree, but forced himself to nod. Right now he was the only person in the police department who believed her roommate had been murdered, and if the crazy vision was right, then there was a murderer in a mask on the loose, and if he didn't figure out how to prove it, more people could die.

The thought sobered him. "Any idea why people might be wearing this mask?"

She pulled in a slow breath and nodded. "Kronos was the leader of the Titans before Zeus trapped them all in the center of the Earth."

"Like *Clash of the Titans*?" He set his pen down. "You think these people believe in this stuff?"

Her back stiffened. "Every myth begins from a need to explain a reality. So while I'm not sure a real Kraken is locked up in the Earth's core, I think it's likely there is some inhuman force there, something imprisoned to keep it from destroying the world."

Nate rocked back in his chair. He wanted to laugh and point out how insane this sounded, but the vision of the robed man in the gold mask reminded him of the danger. Even if this wasn't real, at least one man with a taste for homicide was buying it.

"So this Kronos guy is trapped underground, and you think there's some cult in Crystal City worshipping him?"

"Maybe?" She shrugged. "When Kronos ruled, it's referred to as the Golden Age of Man. All milk and honey. I could see a cult wanting to bring back man's heyday. Maybe they're end-of-the-world junkies." She met his eyes. "And Nia was *not* part of some cult, just in case you were going to ask again."

Her cell phone chimed. She glanced at the text and frowned. "Can you excuse me for a second?"

MEL CALLED POLLY back on her cell as she watched Detective Malone—Nate—jotting notes on his pad. The muscles in his forearm flexed and released as he wrote, and she caught herself nearly starting to drool. She rolled her eyes at herself as Polly answered.

"Hey, Mel. They denied the permit for the roof restoration."

"What?" She lowered her voice. "Why? It was a standard building permit. We're not doing anything crazy."

Polly sighed. "They're sending out a building inspector to check the foundation and the support beams to make sure it's structurally sound before they'll issue the permits. The soonest appointment he had open was next month."

"But we can't start the interior renovations without repairing the holes in the roof. This is going to delay our opening."

"Which may be what they were after from the beginning," Polly grumbled.

Mel frowned. "I was just babbling when I said someone out there doesn't want the Theater of the Muses to open. My typical worst-case scenario; it wasn't real."

"Maybe it's more real than any of us realized." Her voice softened. "Maybe this is why someone hurt Nia."

Mel shook her head. "No one would murder someone to stop a theater from opening. That would be ridiculous."

"I hope you're right." Polly sighed. "I'll keep you posted."

"Thanks," Mel said and then they both hung up.

Mel returned to the table in a fog of questions.

"Everything okay?"

Nate's deep voice snapped her back to reality. "No. Our building permits for the theater are being delayed."

"Why?"

She nodded, suddenly unsure what to say. Talking about the theater hit too close to home, too close to the truth of what connected the sisters, to dreams of changing the world and inspiring future generations.

Nate tapped on the page of Kronos masks again. "Could these people be dressed like this in protest of your theater?"

"I don't think so. How would they even know we're involved in restoring it? We formed an LLC to keep our names and personal property off the project."

Nate picked up his pen again. "Can you give me the name on the permits? I could do some digging and see if I can find out what's really behind the delays. Just to be sure."

It couldn't hurt, could it? She swallowed the lump in her throat. "Our company name is Muses Anonymous, LLC."

He smiled, and a warning light went off in her head. She needed to figure out what really happened to Nia, and intimate relationships never ended well for her. Not to mention that she'd made a no-dating pact with her sisters until the theater opened.

Let this one pass by.

"How'd you guys come up with the name?" he asked.

Oh crap. She never should have told him about the permits. "Polly is funding our project. It was her idea. Like that Theater of the Muses in Paris? That's her vision for the place."

Before he could ask any more questions she wasn't prepared to answer, his cell vibrated on the table.

"Sorry. I've got to take care of this." He lifted his gaze. "Thanks for the information. I'll let you know if I find any leads on your roommate, and I'll see if I can dig anything up on those permits, too."

"Thanks." She sipped her coffee, admiring the view as he walked away. He was clearly still hiding something. She didn't believe for a second that the Kronos masks were part of some big crime spree. Not when she and her sisters were muses. But he didn't know that…did he?

Picking up her red pen, she did her best to focus on grading papers.

Yeah, right.

By the time Nate and John finished questioning eyewitnesses of a hit-and-run in the park, all he wanted was a beer and a bed, but when he got home and had a brew in hand, he didn't head for the television or his bedroom. Instead he sat at the dining room table—his makeshift desk—and opened his notebook and the folder of masks.

Once his laptop fired up, he started searching for information on Kronos and the Titans. A few days ago, he would've laughed his ass off at the idea of Greek gods shoving girls down the stairs in Crystal City, California, but now…

He rubbed his shoulder and winced. If he didn't know better, he'd think he was sunburned, but he hadn't been to the beach in weeks. He got up, unbuttoning his shirt on the way to the bathroom. Twisting around, he couldn't quite see it in the mirror. He grabbed his cell phone and took a picture of the reflection of his back.

He frowned staring at the pic. "What the hell?"

His birthmark on the back of his shoulder had been almost black his entire life, but now… He enlarged the photo. It was bright red and raised—like a brand. He didn't have time for a doctor appointment right now, but it definitely looked angry. Maybe all those years of running on the beach were finally catching up to him. Shit.

He tossed the shirt on the edge of the bed and went back to the table. He still had a case to solve. Greek gods, a theater, and a dead woman shoved down the stairs. There had to be a connection he was missing. If the vision he'd seen was real, what tied Mel and her roommate to this Kronos guy?

He took a swig of beer and scrolled through more

Greek myths about Titans. Maybe he needed a new angle. Mel and her roommate were both part of the Muses Anonymous, LLC. He opened another window and typed *Greek muses* into the search engine. He clicked the first listing on the page.

The more he read, the more the mark on his back ached. Nine muses. How many "sisters" did Mel have in this LLC? He opened another window, logging into the city records. Including the victim, there had been nine. Coincidence. Had to be.

He scanned the names. Nia, the victim, Mel, he'd met Callie. He kept skimming when one popped out at him. Thalia. Unique, and he was almost sure… He switched windows to the page about the Greek muses. Thalia was the Muse of Dance.

He leaned back in his chair and rubbed a hand down his face. This was nuts. He couldn't believe he was even considering this. It had to be a coincidence.

Then he read further and froze. The nine muses were the daughters of Zeus.

Kronos would hate his jailer. What better way to hurt someone than to go after his children?

He got up, pacing the kitchen. This was certifiable. Mel was a high school English teacher, not a daughter of a fictional god. But what if this guy in the Kronos mask didn't see it that way? What if they were real to him?

Mel could be his next target.

He snatched up his phone and dialed her phone

number.

"Hello?"

Just hearing her voice calmed the tempest inside. It made no sense. Every part of him was tense. The urgency filtered into his voice. "Mel, I need to see you right away."

She hesitated. "What's wrong?"

"Face-to-face. It's important."

"Okay." She sounded less than convinced. "Meet me at Gracie's in thirty minutes."

NATE ARRIVED FIRST and nursed a Coke at the bar. Although his back was to the door, he was aware of her presence the second she opened it. How was that even possible?

She took the stool next to him, resting her hands on the bar. "What's so important?"

On an impulse, he placed his hand over hers and braced himself. Nothing. Well. Far from nothing. In fact, his entire body sizzled with need. But he had no visions. He hadn't had any at the hit-and-run earlier, either. Maybe the visions had been a one-time thing. Or a brain tumor.

"Sorry." He pulled his hand away. Thankfully she didn't seem offended, but confusion lined her brow. He got up and pointed toward a corner table. "Let's talk somewhere more private."

He followed her; grateful she didn't mention his inappropriate physical contact.

Once she was seated, her gaze locked on his, her full lips struggling to hold back a smile. "I hope I didn't come down here to hold hands."

He raked his fingers through his short hair. "Sorry about that." He leaned in closer. "Solving crimes is like following a spider web. Everything is connected in some way, it's just figuring out where things intersect so I can find the spider in the middle."

"And did you find it?"

He shrugged. "Is there a reason you didn't mention the Muses were daughters of Zeus?"

Her smile faded. She rested her forearms on the table, leaning closer to him. "You were asking about Kronos, not Zeus."

"Your theater is for the nine Muses, Zeus's daughters. If I were a crackpot on Team Kronos, I'd hit Zeus where it hurts—his beautiful girls." He moved even closer to her, pulled in by some unseen magnetic force, an unquenchable thirst to be near her parching him.

"You might be on to something, Detective Malone." Her breath warmed his lips as she spoke.

"Nate," he whispered. "Call me Nate."

"Nate..." she whispered as she closed the distance between them. Her lips brushed his.

Fireworks erupted behind his eyelids, landscapes rolling through his consciousness in a constant stream he couldn't comprehend. Greece, Rome, Paris, Crystal

City. He pulled back, struggling to clear his head.

"Did you see that?" he asked.

She frowned. "See what?"

Maybe he needed to get more than his birthmark checked out. He ran a hand down his face. "Sorry. When I'm around you…"

"Please don't apologize, you'll hurt my pride." She almost smiled. "And *I* kissed *you*. Just so you know."

He was usually smooth when it came to women, but Mel wasn't like anyone he'd ever met. She threw off his equilibrium, and the crazy visions weren't helping. He shook his head. "I wasn't apologizing for the kiss." He chuckled. "In fact, I'd be willing to try that again sometime."

"Good." She settled back. "I'm sorry I didn't mention the muses had a tie to Zeus."

He swallowed and met her gaze head-on. As much as he was feeling for her, he needed to focus, even if it meant confronting her. "Are you keeping anything else from me that could help with this case, Mel?"

Was she? Mel struggled to string her thoughts together. She shouldn't have kissed him, but besides being the hottest detective she'd ever seen, he was also the only person who believed her and was trying to figure out what really happened to Nia. Knowing someone was going on a limb to help her was a heady sensation as it was, and add in that he smelled like an untamed forest, and her resistance ran really low.

And now that she'd gotten a taste of his lips on hers, she was hard-pressed to focus. "I think I've told you all I can." She tried to keep her voice from trembling, from giving away the truth of who she was, who Nia was.

He pulled out the printout of the masks again. "If there is some kind of cult that worships Kronos, it's not a big leap to think that if they found out you all were restoring a theater for the muses, they'd see hurting you as a way to punish the guy who defeated their leader. People have killed for less."

Could he be right? "But we don't advertise who we are, and our company is an LLC. We don't have our names anywhere on the project. How could they have made that connection?"

"Maybe they saw you coming and going from the theater? That's the part I'm missing." He reached across the small table to take her hand. "But if I'm right, you or one of your sisters could be the next target." He squeezed. "You need to be careful."

She nodded, struggling to convince herself he was wrong. They were muses. They weren't hurting anyone. Why would anyone want them dead?

No. There had to be another explanation. Clio, their resident Muse of History, studied every mention of the muses in any ancient text she could get her hands on. If there were Kronos supporters out there, wouldn't they know?

She shielded her fear with bravado. "I'll keep my eye out for a guy in a gold mask."

He groaned. "This isn't a joke. I don't want to get a call that something's happened to you."

She sobered, glancing down at their joined hands. "Why do you care?"

He caught her chin with his other hand. His gaze demanding she look at him. "Because I lost someone I should've been protecting. I'll never let that happen again."

She searched his eyes and saw raw concern, worry, and regret. Her chest constricted, the memory of Nia's empty stare crawling out of the shadows of her mind. This was real. She needed to circle the wagons. If they put their heads together, she and her sisters would come up with a plan. They had to.

She slid her hand free of his. "I appreciate your concern." She pushed her chair back. "I think I'd better get back to Callie's." She stood, and a scar on his right bicep peeked out from under the sleeve of his T-shirt.

Until now, she hadn't even noticed that he was out of his detective suit. A gentle smile tugged at her lips. "You should wear short sleeves more often."

Before he could respond, she hustled out of the bar. Something was going on. Something big, like the dreams that brought her sisters together. But this time, it wasn't a theater bringing them together. It was a killer tearing them apart.

CHAPTER 5

MEL GROANED. "I kissed him."

Callie pulled out the chair next to her at the long dining room table. "The detective? Seriously? We made a pact."

"I know, I know. But there's something about him."

Callie sighed. "We'll never get this theater open if we're all off chasing men. This is important. Like, *for all mankind and the future of the world* important."

Mel put her hands up. "I get it, Miss Epic Poetry." She shook her head. "He's the only one who believes that Nia's fall wasn't an accident."

"He seems like a good guy, but we need to focus on finding Nia's killer, and then finish the theater. We don't have time for distractions. No men."

"Yeah, yeah, I know." Mel rolled her eyes. "Inspiration before intercourse."

Callie chuckled. "I should put that on a T-shirt."

"He's smart, too." Her voice wavered, fear creeping back into her consciousness. "He thinks he found a link." Releasing a breath, she forced the words out. "We may all be targets."

But before Mel could finish telling Callie about her

meeting with Nate, Clio burst in, books and scrolls in her arms. "Sorry to interrupt, but I think I stumbled onto something interesting."

Mel tensed, already imagining that the Muse of History discovered some ancient prophecy of their demise. She took a deep breath rolling her eyes at herself. *Glass half-full, remember?*

Clio pulled out a chair at the table and sat down, carefully placing her ancient documents on the tabletop. "I was actually looking for some record of previous muses being murdered, and while I didn't find that, I did find this…" She unrolled a scroll, pointing to a few faded lines.

Callie propped her head up on her elbow. "It's all in Greek."

Clio nodded, then sighed. "Sorry. I forgot you can't read it." She tossed her braid over her shoulder and leaned in closer to the text. *"Every generation, the nine daughters of Zeus are reborn, and with their rebirth are also nine Guardians. They will be marked by the gods, and given gifts to protect his treasure. Their abilities will only be unlocked when they find their muse."* She tipped her head up, looking from Mel to Callie. "We have Guardians."

Mel crossed her arms. "Where was Nia's?"

Clio sighed, rolling the scroll up again. "It doesn't say how they find us, just that when they do, their "abilities" will be unlocked."

"A lot of good that does us if we can't find them."

Mel leaned her head back and stared at the ceiling.

"According to the scroll, they're supposed to find us." Clio took her glasses off. "But if the gods thought we needed Guardians, it's possible there has been trouble in the past, too."

Callie got up and took a cup out of the cupboard. "Do you think they have dreams like we all did?"

Clio shrugged. "It didn't say. I'll keep looking. Maybe I can find another reference."

Mel rubbed her forehead. "Better find it quick. Nate thinks there might be a Kronos worshipper out there and he might know who we are."

"What?" Callie came back to the table. "Why would he make a connection like that? How is that possible?"

"He was researching the mask and the myths about the Titans." Mel shrugged, hoping she looked flippant like some of the teens in her classes instead of a guilty five-year-old. "He also offered to check into the delay in our permits, and I might have told him the name of our LLC. Which I guess led him to start researching the muses."

"You didn't." Callie frowned. "Mel, we don't know anything about this guy. The theater, Nia, our calling, this is *our* responsibility."

Mel jumped out of her chair. "I get it, okay? But there's something about him. He wants to help us."

Clio cocked a brow. "That's pretty hopeful for the Muse of Tragic Poetry."

"Right?" Mel shook her head. "I'm telling you,

though—he really could help us. Yes, I don't know him well, but I can tell you he's been shot twice, he respects my teaching abilities, and he believed me when no one else did." A light bulb burst to life over her head. "And I trust him."

That last part was meant to be in her inside voice.

Callie and Clio shared a quiet look before Callie stood. "Maybe he's your Guardian."

"What?" Mel frowned. "Seriously?"

Callie glanced at Clio and back to Mel, then raised her eyebrows. "Well, he could be. You said you felt a connection with him."

She was stretching, but Mel couldn't help but think about the night he took her back to her condo. Something had left him physically shaken up, but he wasn't sharing what. He also came to her with pages of Kronos masks out of the blue. And after she'd kissed him, he asked if she'd *seen* anything.

What did *he* see? Maybe he was seeing visions.

Holy crap. Clio might be on to something.

Mel pointed to the scrolls. "How do I tell if he's *my* guy?"

"Your *Guardian*." Clio slipped her glasses back into place. "All it references is being 'marked by the gods.'"

Mel started to smile. "I guess I'll have to get him naked and check for any markings."

Callie groaned. "Hey, we made a pact."

"That was before we had this information." They both turned toward Clio.

Callie frowned. "What are you saying?"

Clio shrugged. "I think I'm saying if these Guardians find us, there may be a reason we need to keep them close." Then she quickly added, "Maybe he's the key to finding Nia's killer."

"Exactly." Mel nodded. "And once we're safe, he might be able to help us with the theater, too. He did say he would look into helping us get the permits."

Callie threw her hands up. "I give up." She glanced between the two of them. "But *I* intend to keep our pact and stay focused."

"I know, I know. Inspiration before intercourse." Mel chuckled.

Clio giggled, and Callie shot her a glare. "This isn't a laughing matter."

"If we don't laugh, we'd cry. Would that be better?" Mel crossed her arms, her gaze locked on Callie. "We've already lost Nia, and if Nate is right, they could have all our names on a list."

Clio picked up her books. "Why would they want to keep us from opening the theater?"

Mel shrugged. "Nate thinks it's a way to hurt our 'father', to punish him for imprisoning Kronos."

Callie raised a brow. "But you don't think so."

"Zeus isn't exactly around to weep for us. I think there's another reason, and it's got to be connected to the theater. We just need to figure it out."

Callie nodded. "And until then we all should be very careful."

Nate checked his cell while he waited for the doctor to come in. The nurse left him a paper gown but they let him keep his pants on, so covering his chest with the flimsy thing seemed silly. His doctor knew about his scars anyway.

He scrolled through his e-mails and clicked on one from the city planner's office. Nate helped him with a trespassing neighbor a few years back and called in a favor to see if he could figure out who was delaying Mel's building permits.

The reply was simple. There was no paper trail, but the building commissioner's largest campaign donor was Belkin Oil.

Why would an oil company care about restoring a theater? There had to be someone else putting up roadblocks.

The door opened, and he tucked his cell in his pocket.

"Hey, Nate. How're you feeling?"

Dr. Lee had been Nate's general practitioner since high school. If Nate was seriously going crazy, he figured his longtime doctor would be able to tell. And if the thing on his back was skin cancer, maybe he could get it removed while he was here.

"I'm all right. Worried about my birthmark on my back. It looks angry."

The doctor finished with noting something on the chart and pulled on some latex gloves. "Have you been wearing sunscreen when you run?"

Nate nodded. "Yeah. But I usually wear a shirt anyway."

Cold hands on his back had his nipples shrunken to sunflower seeds. Dr. Lee hummed, poking and squeezing. "Does it itch? Have you been scratching it?"

"No, but sometimes it burns."

It started the night he took Mel to the precinct. He frowned. And it got worse when he was researching the connection between the muses and Zeus.

Usually when I'm worried about Melanie Jacoby.

The doctor came around to the other side. "I'm going to give you a referral to a dermatologist. It doesn't look like skin cancer, but it could be some type of rash."

"Thanks, Doc."

While Dr. Lee typed the referral into the computer, Nate rubbed his hands on his pants and forced the words from his mouth. "There's something else, too."

His doctor looked up. "All right."

"I've been having these…visions. Like sometimes I touch something and…see what happened, I think." He shook his head. "Am I losing it?"

Dr. Lee typed something and met his eyes. "Any headaches or blackouts?"

"No."

His fingers tapped the keyboard. "Are the visions

painful?"

"No."

"And you're not falling asleep when they come on?"

Nate chuckled. "Definitely not."

Dr. Lee started typing as he spoke. "I've known you a long time, so I'm going to share something off the record." He crossed his arms and rolled his stool back. "There are things medical science can't explain. Why a father can suddenly find the strength to lift a car off his child, or how a mother can sense when her baby is in danger." He stood up. "A good detective can become very dependent on his intuition, and maybe these visions are an extension of this. Unless you start experiencing pain, blindness, or loss of consciousness, the fact that you recognize that this is irregular tells me that you're not 'losing it.'"

The weight of worry lifted from Nate's shoulders. Until that moment, he hadn't realized how afraid he'd been that he might have had a brain tumor. "Thanks, Doc."

Dr. Lee reached for the door. "The mark on your back is another story. Don't ignore it."

"I'll call the dermatologist."

"See that you do." He smiled and left the room.

Nate put his shirt back on. So he wasn't crazy or dying. But if the visions were real, Mel was in danger, and he had to figure out how to use the visions to help, and fast.

Melanie. He sighed. It seemed to always come back to her. He was teetering on the border of obsession. He ran a hand down his face. This had to stop.

He headed back to his place, eager for a run. He needed to clear his head and think, trace the webs and find the spider wearing the golden Kronos mask.

The beach was crowded, but he popped in his ear buds and the noise faded away. His running playlist had a driving beat to help him keep his pace. He stayed on the boardwalk to keep the sand out of his shoes, and the breeze from the ocean kept him from overheating. The ritual helped, every step brought his mind more in focus.

Why did he only have visions sometimes?

He needed to do more research, but maybe thinking about a crime brought them on, or maybe whatever he touched had a story to tell. But he gripped the torqued wheel of the bicycle at the scene of the hit-and-run and nothing. Then when Mel kissed him, so many places had flashed before his eyes that he couldn't keep up. The connection had to be the muses and that theater.

And it ended in Crystal City.

What was he missing?

He pumped his legs faster, sweat rolling down his face. Shifting his focus, he worked backward from the theater. The building commissioner delayed the permits, and the biggest supporter of his campaign was an oil company. It made no sense. Why would they care about a theater?

The muscles in his calves and thighs began to ache and his side cramped, pain stabbing his lungs. He slowed his stride and lifted his gaze. Goose bumps prickled his arms. He was in the shadows of a rundown theater. He turned around, frowning. How far had he run?

Chest heaving, he crossed the street to the chain-link fence surrounding the building. He never asked Mel for an address. And yet, he ran all the way to the door. Miles. No wonder his legs were like giant sequoias.

He walked the perimeter, scanning the area. There was a "No Trespassing" sign, and a banner for a contractor, but no mention of Muses Anonymous, LLC. So how could this cult—if there even was one—know Mel's roommate had been involved in restoring the theater? Maybe they were watching it, stalking the sisters?

Around the back of the building, a cracked parking lot with faded white lines sat forgotten, except for a single silver sedan at the far corner. He frowned, walking in its direction. Suddenly the engine came to life and the tires squealed as the car raced out of the lot.

He'd only had time to grab the first three numbers on the plate. He pulled out his cell phone and typed in *Silver Honda Accord - 358*. It wouldn't be enough to find the car, but he would at least have a list. It was a starting point.

Not that he had any proof to link that car to the crime. Maybe the driver had been smoking weed and didn't want to be bothered. But they also could have been waiting to see if Mel and her friends were going to show up to work on the building today.

Nate tucked his cell back into his running armband and leaned against the fence to rest. A vision exploded in his head. A man dressed all in black squeezed through a hole in the chain-link. He had a toolbox in his hand.

Then as quick as it came on, the vision was gone.

Nate cased the fence line until he found a clipped opening hiding at a corner post. Just like the vision. Adrenaline laced his bloodstream. He tugged the fencing back and slid inside. Without his badge, he had no business trespassing, so he jogged to a smashed door and disappeared into the shadows. The last thing he needed was to be seen and have someone calling the police.

Not only would his boss hand him his ass on a platter for going in without a warrant or a badge, but John wouldn't leave him alone again if he discovered Nate was still working this case.

Without the lights on inside, his eyes struggled to adjust to the thick shadows. The musty scent added to the atmosphere of dread, putting his senses on high alert. He retrieved his cell and turned on the flashlight app. Cobwebs and dirt lined the rows of seats leading up to the stage. He had no idea what he might be looking for, but if his vision was real, someone else had been in here.

As he reached the front row of seats, his gut twisted into a tight knot. He didn't need a blast of pictures in his head to know something was off; he just needed to spot it. He ran the flashlight beam along the stage and swung it back again. Although most of the stage was covered in dirt and debris, there was a clean spot in the middle.

He was pressing his hands on the stage floor to boost himself up when another vision hit. The man in black. He'd been here. Nate's heart raced. The man opened the case he had been carrying and took out two gray squares of putty.

Explosives.

"Oh shit." His voice echoed through the empty hall.

He hopped up, wishing like hell he had his gun—not that a weapon was going to help him if the building collapsed. He circled the clean area and knelt down to run his fingers over it. There was an edge. He set his phone down, tracing the cut in the floor. The square popped up exposing two blocks of C-4.

He grabbed his phone and called the station. "I need the bomb squad out here now." He told dispatch what he'd found, as well as the cross streets for the theater.

Then he got the hell out of dodge.

The SWAT team rolled up ten minutes later. Nate was at the back of the parking lot when John parked and got out of the unmarked sedan. He stared at the dilapidated theater and then back at Nate. "What in the hell were you doing all the way out here?"

"I went for a run."

He cocked his head, crossing his arms. "And you ran through a hole in a chain-link fence, into an abandoned building, and just happened to pull up the floorboards and find explosives inside?"

"Well, when you say it like that …"

John chuckled and sighed. "Talk to me, Malone. What the hell is up with you?"

Nate shook his head. Even if he understood what was happening, this was one thing he couldn't share with his partner.

"I was running by and noticed an idling car back here. When I approached, they peeled out and drove away. I got a partial on the plate, but I thought I'd better investigate." He cleared his throat. "Any chance you could give me a lift back to my place?"

John pulled off his sunglasses. "You really ran here from your condo? Christ, Malone, that's about fifteen miles. You training for a marathon or something?"

No wonder his legs were like limp spaghetti noodles. "I was trying to figure things out. I guess I lost track of how far I'd come."

"Get in. The bomb squad's got it from here."

CHAPTER 6

THE POLICE DETECTIVE was becoming a problem.

The leader of the Order wasn't going to be pleased. The enforcer carried his toolbox into his tiny apartment and locked the door. He'd barely gotten out of the parking lot unseen, and by the time the detonators were set to go off, the bomb squad had already completed their work.

The theater was still standing, an affront to the Order of the Titans.

If he couldn't take down their precious theater, he would cross another muse off his list. He opened the cupboard by the sink and carefully removed the paper taped under the shelf. Nia was blacked out. Next in line, her roommate, Melpomene. The Muse of Tragic Poetry went by Melanie Jacoby now.

And her demise would definitely be poetic.

He sat in his stark living room envisioning scenarios. He could crack her head with a bat while she graded term papers. Or maybe poison her tea. He rocked in the chair with a warm smile on his face. Time was on his side. Their leader had blocked the building permits on the theater for at least a month. Plenty of time to thin out the herd.

MEL WAITED AT a back table in Gracie's, unable to sit still. Detective Malone, Nate, had discovered explosives planted inside the floor of the stage of the theater. Impossible on many fronts, but somehow he'd found the theater, gotten inside, noticed an uneven floor, and called the bomb squad in before all her and her sisters' work went up in flames.

He was like Superman with a gun.

His broad shoulders filled the doorway as he tugged his sunglasses free. He was in a T-shirt and shorts: tan, muscled, and walking toward her table.

Yeah, the no-dating pact was flying right out the window.

He sat down across from her, but he wasn't smiling. "We have to talk, but not here."

"Okay." She stood and grabbed her messenger bag from the chair. "You told me to meet you here, right?"

He nodded. "So we could meet up. Not to stay here."

He spoke quickly, agitated. Before she could respond, he caught her hand, his fingers lacing with hers, and instead of being shocked or annoyed at his alpha tendencies, her pulse kicked up a notch. She followed him out and across the street toward the shoreline. He donned his shades again and walked her to a bench overlooking the beach.

"We need to lay some cards on the table," he said as he sat.

She stared at his profile, but he didn't turn her way, his bright eyes hidden by his sunglasses. "I'm not sure what you mean."

"I ran to your theater even though I had no idea where it was." He finally turned her way. "How is that possible? And this..." He raised their joined hands. "This is the first time I've been able to breathe in two days."

Mel gnawed at her bottom lip. Could he truly be the Guardian Clio found in the scrolls? It wasn't like she could just ask. But she had to do something. "This is going to sound crazy..."

He gave a soft chuckle. "You wouldn't believe how crazy my life has been since I met you."

"Okay." She pulled her hand free of his, readying herself for him to run. "Do you have some kind of odd *mark* on your body anywhere?"

He slid his sunglasses off, cringing as if she'd suddenly grown a third eye. "A mark?"

"I told you it would sound crazy."

He shook his head, staring at the waves crashing on the sand. Finally, he tensed and faced her again. "Wait a second." He tugged his T-shirt over his head, exposing a rock-hard six-pack. Before she could get a good look, though, he turned the other way, putting his back toward her. He reached around and pointed up to his right shoulder. "I have a birthmark that's been feeling strange. My doctor thinks it might be a rash, but I'm leaning toward skin cancer."

On the back of his right shoulder blade was a crescent of color, like a waxing crescent moon. It was raised and bright red.

"Has it always been this color?" she asked.

He pulled his shirt back down in a hurry. "No." He faced her again, suddenly very close. "It started burning the night I met you."

It *was* him. Her Guardian. He had to be.

She swallowed the lump in her throat. "Have you noticed anything else strange since we met?"

A muscle jumped in his cheek, his green eyes cold. "My cards are on the table. I showed you the mark. Now tell me what it means. Does this have anything to do with how I ended up at your theater even though you never told me where it was?"

"I don't know, but it probably has to do with the mark." She lowered her voice. "You're a Guardian."

"I'm a police detective."

Mel sighed. "Yes, you are, but being a Guardian means you have a latent ability that only surfaces if you find your muse." She pressed her lips together, trying to recall the exact wording. "Clio found a scroll that mentioned Guardians, mortal men marked by the gods to protect the daughters of Zeus. When he finds his muse, his abilities are revealed. Or something. That's not the exact translation."

He opened his mouth to speak and stopped, then shook his head. "You're telling me you're my muse?"

She nodded slowly. "It seems that way."

"Like, seriously a muse?" A humorless chuckle escaped his lips. "You look damn good for your age."

"No, it's not like that."

"Then what is it *like* exactly?" His shoulders tensed. "I think I have the right to know."

She braced herself and forced out the words. "I didn't know until I was eighteen. I started having dreams of all the Theaters of the Muses throughout the centuries, and the final one was here in Crystal City. So then I had to come here. I was compelled, I guess. Obsessed. Anyway, when I got here, I found my sisters. There were nine of us, and each of us had dreams that led us to the condemned theater."

"So your dad isn't a Greek god?"

"No. But after we found each other, we compared notes and learned we were all having the same dreams. Crazy, right?" Mel sighed. "Aspects of our personalities were enhanced by the muse inside of us, too."

She waited for him to reply or ask a question, but his silent investigator stare continued.

She cleared her throat. "Anyway, Clio could read Greek and started researching. There are ancient stories about the muses being reborn to each generation. We're charged with inspiring mankind to move forward—inventions, music, and science. We can change the world. So we all settled here, bought the theater, and now we're trying to restore it."

Nate rested his hands on the edge of the bench, leaning toward the waves as if he was going to bolt at any minute. "So I was drawn there, too?"

"As I understand it. Each Guardian is a mortal man, just like us, but he has a muse to protect and a 'gift' to help protect her, but it doesn't present itself until he finds his muse. Honestly, I don't know how this works. Maybe you were pulled there to stop the explosion, to protect us. Or me…"

"Shit." He pressed his lips together and blew out a pent-up breath. "And how was I picked for this detail?"

Mel frowned. The prophecy hadn't mentioned unwilling Guardians. It hadn't occurred to her that he wouldn't want the responsibility.

Just when he was starting to make her believe the glass might be half-full…

"Supposedly you were marked by the gods from birth," she explained quietly.

"They picked the wrong guy." He got up and walked along the sand, his back to her.

Mel's heart hammered so hard she had to rub at the ache. She knew it was a lot to drop on someone. She didn't blame him for running as fast as he could the other way. But she hated to admit that she was disappointed. At least Callie would be glad to know their pact was still intact.

Mel got up and quietly went to crosswalk at the corner. Her car was parked at Gracie's across the way.

She reached to press the button when a large hand caught her wrist.

Nate's deep voice teased her senses. "Where are you going?"

She dropped her hand and stared up at him. "You said you were the wrong guy. I thought we were done. I'm not going to force you to help us."

"Wow." He rocked back, shaking his head with a humorless chuckle. "Forgive me for not embracing this insanity instantly. Give me a few minutes to think this through." His tone softened a little. "I'm not turning my back on you."

She pulled her hair back from her forehead, staring at her shoes. "I guess I should probably tell you that the muse that awakened in me is the Muse of Tragic Poetry." She tentatively peered up at him. "Jumping to the worst-case scenario is sort of my go-to since I turned eighteen."

Nate laughed, a real, warm laugh that sent heat all the way down to her toes. "That's why you teach high school poetry."

Mel elbowed him playfully and walked back over to the bench without looking back to see if he was following her. He took a seat beside her, and his smile faded.

"When I took you home the other night, I touched the light switch and saw a man's hand in a black glove turning it off. I thought I imagined it until I leaned on the banister and another vision showed up. In that one, a man wearing a black robe and a gold Kronos mask shoved your roommate down the stairs." He brought a hand up to trace along the edge of her jaw. "I didn't want you to be next."

Her pulse jumped at his tender caress. "Psychometry. You touch things and see what happened. Your gift."

He sighed and pulled away, leaving her aching for his touch again. "I wouldn't call it that exactly. It doesn't work all the time, and I can't figure out how to turn it on."

"Maybe it only activates if there's been violence."

He straightened up and met her eyes. "No. When we kissed the other night, I saw all the cities, all the Theaters of the Muses, and it ended here in Crystal City." He took her hand. "It's you. The visions have to be connected to the muses, don't they? That's why I saw your roommate's killer and not the hit-and-run driver the other day. The injured bicyclist wasn't a muse."

Okay, he was smart, too. Not only did he have a chiseled body and a scar, but with his intelligence and his ability to make connections, he would've been her type even if he weren't sporting a mark from the gods.

She nodded, refocusing. "Maybe that's what drew you to the theater."

"Maybe? Once I got there and touched the fence, I saw a man in black sliding through an opening. The rest was instinct, I guess."

Her stomach chose that moment to remind them

both that they hadn't eaten dinner. Nate grinned and stood up, offering his hand. "Think they still have a table for us?"

She took his hand, savoring the sizzle. "Only one way to find out."

MEL'S EYES SPARKLED as she discussed her students. She may have been the Muse of Tragedy, but she had no trouble laughing and obviously loving her kids and her work. Nate had a soft spot for kids. It was the relationships that led to children that were a problem. His alcoholic father had beaten his capacity for love and trust—of adults, at least—out of him.

The scar on his arm from the bullet wound was the least of the battle wounds covering his body. Cuts from broken beer bottles, cigarette burns, and gashes from being shoved to the ground made him into a canvas of abuse, a reminder to him that trust and dependency only brought pain.

Maggie's toothless grin filled his head. She had depended on him, and look where it got her. He sipped his soda and forced himself to focus on Mel.

"Did you want to be a teacher before you found your...muse?"

"Yeah. I think so." She shrugged. "I always loved to write, but I'm too social to be a writer for a living. Hours of being alone at a keyboard would make me nuts. Plus, I like kids. There's a moment when they finally grasp a concept and you can almost see it in their eyes."

She sat back against her chair and smiled. "It's a high to know you inspired someone."

"I can imagine." He could also get used to seeing her smile.

"So what about you? Did you always want to be a policeman?"

Too close to home. He cleared his throat and shrugged. "I don't know. I was always tangling with the bullies in school. I wasn't a big guy then, but I did what I could to keep them away from the smaller kids. I never understood picking on someone just because you could."

He ground his teeth, refusing to allow his father to ruin his night. He grabbed the check. "Are you still staying with your friend?"

She nodded.

"She was a firecracker. What's her muse?"

"I'm going to start calling her that." Mel laughed. Jesus, he wanted to hear more of that. "Callie's the Muse of Epic Poetry."

He chuckled. "All five feet of her?"

"Right?" Mel grinned. "Obviously the gods have a sense of humor."

They definitely had a *twisted* sense of humor when they marked him as a Guardian and then sat back and let him get the shit beat out of him by his own father.

But he kept that to himself. He walked her to her car and stopped at the door. "I'm still trying to wrap my head around all of this."

"I know." She stared up at him from under dark lashes. "Can I tell you something?"

"Sure."

Her lips curved at the corners like a shy smile. "I liked you way before I saw the mark on your shoulder."

Without thinking, he bent to brush his lips to hers. She returned the kiss, her mouth soft and slow against his. He slid his arms around her waist, drawing her tight to his body. She fit perfectly in his arms. His pulse shot below his belt until his erection pressed against her, aching for more.

He tasted her lips with his tongue, and she opened to him. The moan that escaped her nearly undid him. He pressed her back against the car, bringing one hand up into her hair, tangling his fingers in the silky strands.

Her hands wandered lower, gripping his ass. He rocked his hips against her, his desire overriding rational thought until she broke the kiss, breathless. "Take me to your place."

He didn't hesitate. He grabbed her hand and hustled her to his car. The drive was a blur, like he couldn't breathe until he had her back in his arms. He kissed her again as soon as she got out.

"Malone!"

Cold shower. He turned around to find John jogging toward him. He stared at Mel for a second, and then narrowed his eyes at Nate. "Am I interrupting?"

His tone made it plain that he knew damned well he was fucking interrupting. Nate took a step away from Mel. "We ran into each other, and I gave her an update on the case. You remember Melanie Jacoby. Mel, this is my partner, Detective Gilman."

John shook her hand, his tense expression unchanged. "Good to see you again. I'm sorry for your loss."

Mel released his hand, crossing her arms. "Thank you. I'm choosing to focus on finding her killer instead of her loss."

John raised a brow. "There's no evidence of a killer. Didn't you tell her, Malone? The ME ruled it an accidental death."

Why was John being such a dick? Nate frowned. "Why are you here?"

"You weren't answering your cell phone. We got a potential lead on the C-4 in the theater."

Shit. He hadn't even looked at his cell phone during dinner. "Let me grab my badge." He turned to Mel. "Sorry about this. I'll drop you back at your car in a minute." He glared at John. "Don't be an asshole."

John smirked. "I'll do my best."

CHAPTER 7

MEL WAITED ON Nate, half expecting his partner to arrest her. It wasn't a crime to make out with a detective, but judging by his partner's reaction, she'd definitely offended him in some way.

"Sleeping with him isn't going to bring your friend back," he said, keeping his attention on the gate to the condos that Nate had just gone through.

She put a hand on her hip. "Excuse me?"

He glanced her way and then back to the gate. "Nate's a good detective. He knows better than to get involved with a witness."

"So I must be seducing him?"

He shrugged. "You tell me." He finally met her eyes. "What's your endgame?"

"Is it so shocking that I think Nate is a great guy?"

A flash of concern lined his eyes before his stern law enforcement mask settled back into place. "I just don't want to see him getting tangled up with a witness, and when things go south, I don't want to see her reporting him to the department."

Mel sighed. A tiny part of her had to respect that John was protecting his partner, but still... "You just assume it'll 'go south' and you don't even know me. Nice."

"I know Nate. Women fall all over him, and they're hurt when he walks. You were a witness he questioned. He shouldn't risk it with you."

Mel crossed her arms. Tightly. "You're warning me that he gets around?"

Nate opened the gate, dressed in his standard slacks and button-down shirt. His holster was a new addition, too.

John lowered his voice. "I'm warning you that he doesn't do relationships, so if you're going into it with that hope, don't be pissed later."

"You're still here." Nate walked up.

"Just chatting with Ms. Jacoby."

Nate looked at them both before raising a brow to his partner. "Were you being an asshole?"

"No more than usual." John met her eyes, and finally he nodded. "Nice seeing you again." He went to his car, calling over his shoulder. "I sent you a text with the address, Malone."

"Be right behind you."

Mel got back in Nate's car, her mind spinning. Nate hadn't given her the "player" vibe at all, but the first thing he'd said when she told him about Guardians was that the gods picked the wrong guy. Maybe the relationship thing his partner mentioned was hidden in Nate's comment.

She stared out the passenger window, digesting Detective Gilman's information. She'd had her share of heartbreaks over the years, and her most recent had come right before she'd moved to Crystal City. It had made making the no-dating pact with her sisters an easy choice at the time.

But heartbreak was part of what made relationships a thrill—taking that risk. She didn't usually shy away. The rush of emotion—the feeling of free falling—made diving in for another chance worthwhile.

Or maybe that was her muse hungering for more tragedy.

"You're really quiet. Did John say something to upset you?" He glanced her way, then back to the street. "He really is a good guy, but he's protective."

Mel reached across to rest her hand on his thigh. "He's definitely that. He told me you're not a relationship guy and if I get angry and report you, you could get in trouble with the department because you questioned me as a witness."

He rested a hand over hers. "Ever since I met you, keeping it professional has been practically impossible."

"So it's true."

"Which part?"

"You could get in trouble for seeing me."

He raised her hand to his lips, brushing a kiss to her knuckles. "I can handle a little trouble. How about you?"

Scars and a thrill seeker. Gods help her...

She smiled, looking over at him. "No risk, no reward, right?"

He squeezed her hand and released it as he pulled into the parking lot behind Gracie's. He parked beside her car and turned to her. "I need to chase down this witness with John. Can I call you later?"

Mel nodded. "I'd like that."

"Good." His smile faded. "Until I find out who was trying to blow up the theater, I'm going to assume it's connected to your roommate's attacker. Stay with Callie. Be safe."

She opened the door. "I will."

Mel got in her car and turned on the engine and the headlights. Nate waited, and then followed her out of the lot. He may not have thought he'd be a good pick for a Guardian, but he was dead wrong.

HE WALKED DOWN the white runner toward their leader. His robed brothers and sisters cheered his approach, encouraging him forward. His breath echoed behind the thick mask. When he reached the platform, he removed the hood of his robe. Their leader anointed his head with oil before placing a laurel wreath over his hair.

He turned to face the Order. They were a small group, twelve souls representing the twelve original Titans. And with their help, the children of Gaia would once again be free and bring about the Golden Age of Man. No more human wars or strife. No egos, no famine, only milk and honey.

But first they needed to stop the daughters of Zeus. The muses could inspire the human race, bringing about new technologies that would eliminate the need to dig into the earth's core, into the prison in which Kronos had been trapped by his own son.

The cheers quieted, and their leader spoke. "Children of Gaia, Mother Earth calls us to free her son."

More cheers.

"Our brother has brought us one step closer to the goal. The Muse of Astronomy is no more." Their leader took his wrist and raised it high like a prizefighter as he drank in the praise.

"There is more to do, but we are moving the Order of the Titans forward. The Golden Age of Man will return, and we will be heralded as heroes of mankind."

He turned to face their leader and tipped his head down with reverence. When he straightened, he descended to join his brothers and sisters. Beside the platform was a stack of wood and twigs with twelve torches circling it. The members of the Order spaced themselves so they each stood behind one of the twelve torches.

Their leader looked up at the night sky, calling to the heavens. "We send our victory to Uranus, Father Sky. Soon his children will be free."

He took up his torch in time with the others, lifting

the flame above his head and awaiting the final signal from their leader.

"Brothers and sisters of the Order of the Titans, tonight we celebrate with sky and earth."

All the torches touched the dry wood. Sparks flew into the night as the fire consumed it, and the black smoke rose up like a serpent. He smiled behind his mask.

With a taste of accomplishment in his mouth, he vowed to continue his work until the muses were no longer a threat to their mission. He would become a hero for all time.

Mel walked through the door to find all her sisters gathered in the circle around Callie's round dining room table like King Arthur's knights. "Wow, did I miss my invitation?"

Callie rolled her eyes. "This is why we made the pact. While you were out on a *date*, the rest of us were here trying to figure out how to keep the theater safe until we can get it finished."

Mel took a seat. "So I guess you aren't even curious about the Guardian prophecy Clio found?"

They all turned her way, and Clio grinned. "It's true, isn't it?"

"Seems to be." Mel glanced around the circle. "Nate has a birthmark on the back of his shoulder. He said it started burning when he met me, and it appears his gift is psychometry. We think it only works if the thing he touches is related to the muses—mainly, to me."

"I *knew* it was true. It's so romantic." Clio placed a hand over her heart.

Callie rolled her eyes. "Some of us don't need to be guarded, thank you very much."

Mel chuckled. "Not to rain on your parade, Clio, but that prophecy doesn't say anything about loving us, just protecting us. It's not like that birthmark wakes up undying love."

Clio sobered, her shoulders slumping a little. "So you guys aren't dating?"

Mel mentally smacked herself. Sometimes being the Muse of Tragic Poetry made it tough to be a good friend.

"There's definitely an attraction there, but there's a better than average chance it'll blaze in like an inferno and then fizzle out." Although she always expected the worst, saying the words out loud actually sort of hurt. She didn't want them to be true.

"The sooner it fizzles out, the sooner we'll have your full attention again. We've got work to do." Callie poked at the blueprints in the center of the table. "Distractions could cost us everything. Nia wanted this as much as any of us. We need to finish what she helped us start."

Mel tried to focus on the discussion of hiring security guards, putting up cameras, and starting a list of potential Titan sympathizers, but her mind kept wandering to Nate. She usually jumped boldly into new relationships, recognizing they wouldn't last, but this regret was new. Diving into this could hurt her. She really liked this guy.

For once, this might be more tragedy than I can take.

Nate sat across from the dockworker while John stood a few feet back from the table. Nate would be the 'good cop' this time, and John would be the intimidator if needed.

"I told you all I know," the guy said.

Nate skimmed his notes. "Two shipments of explosives checked in at the port, one for Ace Demolitions and the other for?"

"It's not on the list?"

Nate lifted his gaze. "But you already knew that didn't you?"

His eyes widened in mock surprise. "I didn't know. It must've been a mistake."

Nate frowned. "Don't you have to check the purchase orders and packing slips?"

"Sometimes."

John approached like a shark smelling blood in the water. "You're telling us you let two shipments of explosives into Crystal City without checking the documents?"

The dockworker recoiled, crossing his arms. "I checked 'em."

"Good." Nate picked up his pen. "So who picked them up?"

The guy chuckled. "I look at a hundred purchase orders and packing lists a day. I can't remember a list that came in last week."

Nate went for the kill. "We didn't tell you it came in last week." He got up from the chair, staring the guy down. "If you can remember that, maybe you can tell us who paid you to keep quiet?"

"Please…these people…" he stammered. "They'll come after me. I needed the money. My wife lost her job."

"I don't care why you're doing it," Nate said.

John placed his hands on the table, leaning in. "But we can protect you if you give us names."

Nate's gut twisted. He'd made that promise of protection once before, and then he'd found her dead body.

"Some guy named Lewis Gold came to the dock and paid me a grand to let him know when the C-4 arrived instead of logging it in the book. I think he worked for Belkin Oil."

Nate jotted down the name. "Thanks for your cooperation. Detective Gilman will help you with paperwork for police protection in case of proseccution."

He left the interrogation room. Rationally, he understood that protection from the department was usually successful, but making those kind of promises still sickened him. They were far from infallible. And failure led to Maggie losing her mother on his watch.

He rolled his shoulders back, struggling to box the memories back up. At least now he had a name. It could lead to a dead end, but it was another thread to chase.

John came over to his desk. "You okay?"

"Yeah."

"You couldn't get out of that room fast enough."

He sighed and looked up at his partner. "I don't feel good offering our protection like it's a blank check for safety."

John shook his head. "This isn't an abusive ex-husband."

"I know." Nate nodded. "I'm fine. Really."

John pulled a chair over. "You going to follow up with Belkin or you want me to do it?"

"You can take the lead over there. I'm going to cross-reference the partial plate and see if I can find a Lewis Gold on the title of a silver Honda Accord."

"All right." John grabbed his coat and paused. "I'd be a bad partner if I didn't warn you off the Jacoby woman."

"Her name is Melanie." He lifted his gaze to his partner. "And it's really none of your business."

"You questioned her on a case. What're you going

to do when you're finished with this one and she goes to the captain and tells him you took advantage of her?"

John's advice was solid, but for some reason it rubbed Nate the wrong way. He stood up, knowing he had a couple of inches on his partner. "She's not that kind of person."

"Because you've known her so long, right?" He shook his head. "There are less dangerous ways to get some tail."

He turned to go, but Nate grabbed his arm. "Don't ever call her that."

"You don't seem okay to me." John glanced at Nate's hand and then back to his face, frowning. "Not by a long shot."

Nate let go and stepped back. What the hell was wrong with him? He cleared his throat. "I appreciate your concern."

John nodded. "Just be careful, okay?"

"I will." He sat at his desk and rubbed his shoulder. His equilibrium was off. Why had John's comment gotten under his skin like that? His partner knew him better than anyone, and Nate didn't do relationships. Not really.

But something about hearing him refer to Mel as "some tail" pissed him off.

So what exactly was she?

His muse.

His.

He groaned and grabbed the DMV list from the partial plate search. This was a problem he could potentially solve. He stuffed the papers into his bag and got in his car.

But instead of going to his condo, he ended up on Lothlórien Lane. He parked on the street and smacked his steering wheel. Being a Guardian was apparently very similar to being a stalker.

His cell phone buzzed. He pulled it out and found a text.

Across the street.

He looked up and Mel waved from the sidewalk in front of her friend's place. She jogged over as he lowered his window.

"Fancy meeting you here." She rested her elbows on the door.

"I was going home. Not really sure how I got here." God, that sounded pathetic. He shook his head. "Are you all right? Maybe that's why I was drawn over here. I've never been much of a stalker."

"So your partner told me."

He frowned. "What'd he tell you?"

"That you're not a commitment kind of guy." She shrugged. "He really *is* protective of you."

Nate nodded, pressing his lips together. "He damn sure is." He pointed at the house. "Everything okay in there?"

She glanced over her shoulder. "Yeah. My sisters

are brainstorming plans to keep the theater safe when we're not there."

"Good. Security cameras would be a step in the right direction." The awkward conversation was killing him. He reached up, slid his fingers into her hair, and pulled her in closer. His lips fused to hers, and she hummed into the kiss, resting her forehead against his.

"You should invite me into your car."

He grinned. "Want to go to my place?"

She stole another kiss and whispered, "Definitely."

CHAPTER 8

THIS TIME THEY made it inside his condo without any interruptions. Good thing, too. He'd had more than his fair share of booty calls, but he'd never wanted anyone as urgently as he wanted this woman. It wasn't just that Mel's body fit perfectly in his arms or that her hungry kisses set him on fire. She fed a part of him he'd sworn had died years ago.

In spite of her tendency toward worst-case scenarios, she didn't live her life safe. There was a flame inside her, a rebel—and something more.

She popped the last two buttons off his shirt. The plastic disks landed on the hardwood floor behind him, and then her top did, too. He kissed his way down her neck as her fingertips glided down his back. Her touch had him aching for more.

He unfastened her bra, his lips trailing lower until he took her nipple into his mouth, circling the tip with his tongue. She gripped his ass tighter, and he rocked his hips against her, his erection making it plain how much he wanted her. Moving to the other nipple, he teased her with his teeth until she gasped his name. It had never sounded sexier.

Shit. He needed her. Now.

He claimed her lips again and scooped her up into his arms. She laughed into the kiss as he carried her to his dark bedroom. He laid her on the bed, whispering, "We have way too many clothes on."

She caught his bottom lip in her teeth. "Couldn't agree more."

He needed her naked before he came with his pants still on. His lips trailed down her chest tasting her skin as he popped the button on her jeans and slowly lowered the zipper. Her fingers tightened in his hair, encouraging him lower. He'd never been more eager.

Desire burned like fire in his veins. He wanted to explore every part of her body, to hear her call out his name, and make her *his*. Most of all, he wanted to lose himself, to drown in their passion in this moment. No tomorrow. Just now.

He tugged her pants off and knelt beside the bed before pulling her down to him, resting her knees over each of his shoulders. The inside of her thighs were soft against his face, reminding him that he should have shaved, but in a million years he hadn't guessed he'd be right here tonight.

He nibbled his way up her inner thigh and slowly licked her opening. Her hands tugged at his hair as her hips writhed under him. He hummed and explored her with his tongue, enjoying the way she moved against him. If he didn't get his damn pants off soon, though, he was going to bust through the damned zipper. And once he discovered her sweet spot, he teased it mercilessly with his tongue while he used his hands to get free of his slacks.

She cried out, "Don't stop!"

Not a chance. He slid a finger inside her, and another, and suddenly her thighs tightened around his head, her entire body trembling. He slowed his attention until the aftershocks diminished. While she struggled to catch her breath, he kissed his way back up her body.

She tugged gently at his hair, pulling him up to her. "Hope you don't think I'm finished with you yet."

IN THE DIM light filtering in from the hallway, she nibbled at his neck, whispering against his skin. "Probably should have asked you earlier…"

"Condoms in the nightstand."

She nipped at his shoulder. "I'll get it."

As she reached for the bedside lamp, he caught her hand. "Let me."

While he opened the drawer, she ran her fingers all the way down his body, stroking his erection until he groaned, his hips working into her rhythm.

She smiled, licking his nipple hard and slow. "Distracted?"

He groaned in answer, his hand still searching the drawer. "You do make it tough to concentrate."

"Good." She stroked him a little faster.

He tore open the plastic, and now it was her turn to stop him. "Let me." She unrolled the condom over his pulsing shaft and kissed his lips.

He gripped her hips tightly. "I need you," he whispered, and her heart pounded in answer.

She rose up over him and slowly settled onto his erection, moaning as each inch of him filled her, enjoying every second.

"Made for me," he growled beneath her.

Mel rested a hand on either side of his head, slowly grinding her hips against his. "I was thinking the same thing."

His hands moved up her back, pulling her close to him. She moaned as her breasts pressed against this bare chest. He rolled her over working his hips into her faster, harder. Her nails dug into his back as their tongues tangled, wrestling almost as urgently as their bodies.

He gasped between urgent kisses. "Can't…get…close…enough."

She clung to him as he slid his hand between them, rubbing her with every thrust. "Come with me."

Mel trembled in his arms as her muscles tightened around him, peaking as he slammed into her deeper. He called her name and froze, his orgasm claiming his body.

Finally, he kissed her lips, tender, slow, and lingering as the aftershocks swept through them. "Give me a second," he whispered.

He got up, slowly separating their bodies and stepped into the bathroom. A minute later he was beside her in the bed. She rested her head on his chest, taking comfort in the steady beat of his heart. He kissed her hair. "That was…"

"Amazing."

He chuckled. "Glad you agree."

Her entire body was relaxed, and being in his arms made it easy to hide from the loss of Nia and the danger lurking around her and her sisters. Her eyes drifted closed and suddenly popped open again. "Do you need to take me back to Callie's place?"

His fingers stopped their lazy circles on her back. "I can if you want to go back there."

She lifted her head to try to see his face in the dim light. "She knows I'm with you. I just thought…"

"What John said was true." He sighed. "I don't believe in relationships, so if it's easier to go…"

The muse inside of her ached for tragedy, to swing into action and yank her clothes on while she stormed out the door; but for once, she shut it out and kissed him. Her lips lingered on his, and finally, she whispered, "I'll stay if you want me to."

Nate stared up into her eyes without saying a word. Maybe she misread him and he'd been trying to get her to agree to leave, but she swore his body language was telling her to sleep over.

He reached up to tuck a lock of her hair behind her

ear and caressed her cheek. "Stay."

She searched his eyes. "You're sure?"

"Yeah." He nodded slowly as his lips started to curve. "I'm not through with you yet."

Mel gasped, her eyes popping open. How many times would her dreams be haunted by Nia being shoved down the stairs? She didn't have any tears left to cry, but that didn't seem to stop the nightmares.

She stretched, her body deliciously sore all over, and turned to find Nate still snoozing. He was on his back with one arm covering his eyes and the sheet lying over his waist like a loincloth. The scar on his bicep caught her eye. She kissed it gently, but as she pulled back, her smile faded.

Wiping her eyes, she scanned his torso again. In the stark morning sunlight, she counted eight round burns spread randomly across his chest. Farther down his abdomen was an ugly scar—definitely not the precision of a surgeon. Her chest constricted as she stared at his sleeping face. Who did this to him?

She rested her head over his heart, and he stirred, lowering his arm to hold her close. Suddenly, he flinched, wide-awake.

"Shit. Sorry." He shook his head.

"Not used to waking up with company?"

He chuckled, kissing her hair. "Something like

that."

She ran her hand up his chest, over three of the burns. Was this why he'd left the lights off last night? Was he sensitive about them?

He twisted to see the clock. "Are you hungry?"

"Yeah." She sat up. "Do you have time to eat before you go to work?"

He nodded. "I brought work home with me. What about you?"

"It's Saturday. No school." She offered a halfhearted cheer and a fist pump.

Nate laughed. "Now *that's* some tragic cheering."

"I aim to please." She leaned over to kiss his forehead. "I don't have my toothbrush or clean clothes or…well, anything."

"Tell you what." He sat up beside her. "If you'll start breakfast, I'll run to the store and grab some toiletries for you. Can you cook?"

Mel smiled. "Yeah, that sounds great."

"Perfect." He got out of bed, exposing a few scars on his back and legs, too. He pulled on some sweatpants and a T-shirt and stepped into the bathroom.

Mel wandered over to his closet and selected a black dress shirt for her morning ensemble. She had it almost buttoned all the way when Nate came out of the bathroom and froze.

She cringed. "Do you have a thing about someone wearing your clothes? Sorry. I should have asked first."

"No, it's not that." He swallowed and shook his

head as a crooked smile crept onto his face. "If this is your ploy to get me back here fast, it's definitely going to work." He crossed the room and pulled her into his arms, one hand sliding up her leg and under the shirt to cup her ass. "You are so sexy."

Mel grinned. "If I didn't have morning breath, I'd kiss you."

He laughed, pressing his lips to her forehead. "I'll be right back." As he headed to the door, he called over his shoulder, "And I'll be collecting that kiss."

Mel wandered into his kitchen and opened the fridge. Food, or lack thereof, could tell you a lot about a person. He had the typical "man staples"—bacon, milk, eggs, a hunk of cheddar cheese, a little bit of butter—but the bottom shelf made her laugh. There was an open package of sour gummy worms. Cute.

She took out the eggs and bacon and went to work. When Nate came through the front door twenty minutes later, the bacon was almost done and she was whipping up the scrambled eggs.

He put a shopping bag on the counter and grinned. "Smells like heaven in here."

"Why, thank you." She poured the eggs into the frying pan and handed him a spatula. "Can you cook these while I clean up?"

He took the spatula and smiled, and she headed for the bedroom, only stopping once to see if he was watching her ass wiggle under his shirt.

He chuckled. "I'd have to be dead not to look."

"I'm glad to see you're in good health." She grinned.

When she met him at the table not long after, he collected on the kiss and took a few more on credit. Then she munched on some bacon while he explained the list he'd be scouring for partial plates of silver Honda Accords owned by Lewis Gold.

"Hopefully I'll find something, but if I were paying off a dockworker to bring in explosives, I'd give him a fake name."

"Did you check to see if Belkin Oil employs a Lewis Gold?"

"John's handling that part." He polished off his eggs and took the plates to the sink.

He rinsed them off and put them in the dishwasher while Mel tried to figure out how to broach the subject of the scars. Would he be angry if she mentioned them? He had to know she saw them when he was getting dressed today. Maybe they were no big deal.

"You didn't tell me you have so many scars in addition to the gunshot to your bicep."

Oh very smooth. She refrained from smacking her own forehead.

He closed the dishwasher and stared into the sink. "No, I didn't."

She swallowed the lump in her throat. "Sorry. It's none of my business."

Nate sat down beside her. "I'm some Guardian, right?"

At least he was still talking and not rushing her out the door. "Maybe I should've told you why I find scars sexy."

"Because most of them are the result of a tragedy?"

"Touché." She chuckled. "But no." She rolled up her sleeve, exposing a scar on her elbow. "I got this running to elementary school. I was going to be late and I freaked, and in my rush, I fell and skidded into school. After it healed and the scab came off, I had this scar and constantly whined to my dad that it was ugly." She lowered her arm. "He told me that I should be proud because scars mean you took a risk and you survived. I think they're sexy because they show you're a survivor."

He got up and crossed to the kitchen window, resting his forearm on the sill above his head. Her stomach twisted. She probably pushed too hard. He'd said he didn't believe in relationships, and maybe this was part of it—real intimacy and vulnerability.

She was getting sick of maybes.

"My dad was an alcoholic." His voice was quiet. "He and my mom fought all the time. I'd get in the middle to try to protect her and he'd beat me…or burn me. He said the burns would leave a mark to remind me that I was nothing."

For a second, her heart clenched. Tears welled in her eyes. "Your dad was full of shit."

He chuckled but didn't turn around. "Yeah."

She got up and stood behind him, sliding her arms

around his waist. "I'm not sure what to say, so this is me trying to tell you I don't care about those scars. They don't mark you as anything but strong in my eyes."

He slowly turned around and held her tight, leaning his cheek on top of her head. His voice was deep and rough. "I've never met anyone like you."

She smiled against his chest. "You're not the first to tell me that."

"I didn't mean it in a bad way." He stepped back and tipped her chin up until she met his eyes. "That wasn't a glass-half-empty compliment." He glanced out the window, swallowed, and pulled his gaze back to her face. "It's seriously scaring me shitless how much I like spending time with you, even outside the bedroom."

Her heart pounded, but the tenuous honesty, the fear in his voice, made it clear he was trying not to run. If she wasn't careful, he'd be out the door.

She rose on her tiptoes and brushed a slow kiss to his lips. "This doesn't have to be a relationship, okay? Just let me be your muse."

He bent to taste her again and smiled. "And I'll be your Guardian."

And for now, that was enough.

CHAPTER 9

Ted Belkin stared out at the bay from his high-rise office window, seething.

Marion opened the door behind him. "Ben is here, Mr. Belkin."

"Send him in."

Footsteps and then the couch cushion sighed. Once the door closed, Ted spun around, his voice a viper's whisper. "A police detective was here this morning. In *my* office. Because of *your* incompetence."

Ben didn't even have the decency to look guilty, the bastard.

"I gave the dockworker a false name. They won't be able to connect me or the explosives to Belkin Oil directly."

Ted smacked the engraved pen set on his desk, sending it careening across the room. It crashed into the wall, and Ben flinched. 'Bout damned time. Ted narrowed his eyes. "You think you have my father's support, but *I'm* blood. Not you. It'll take more than pushing a muse down a flight of stairs to get him to cover your ass with the police."

Ben crossed his legs, his cool demeanor back in

place. "Last time I checked, you brought me into the Order. If I go down and the Order is exposed, I think the responsibility falls to your shoulders, am I right?"

Ted clenched his fists. "Are you trying to blackmail me?"

"No." Ben opened his hands. "Should I?"

Ted huffed out a breath and sat behind his desk. "You better hope the police don't find out your real name."

"If they do, you'll need to call in some favors with your elected officials or get your own hands dirty to complete the mission yourself. That doesn't really seem like your style, though, does it?" Ben stood. "Are we finished here?"

Ted glared up at him. "Treading on thin ice here, Ben. You're not the only person who wants to bring back the Golden Age of Man."

He stopped at the door and turned back. "No, but I *am* the one who can get it done."

MEL WAVED GOOD-BYE as Nate drove down Callie's street. She'd spent the morning helping him comb through the DMV records, but there was no sign of a Lewis Gold connected to a Honda Accord with the first three digits of the license plate he'd seen in the theater parking lot.

Another dead end.

She would've been fine spending the rest of the day with him, but he had a "thing" in the afternoon. Vague…

She knew one hot night together didn't make them a couple, but that didn't quiet the curiosity. He'd been pretty clear about his no-relationship boundary. There was no one to blame but herself if she let it bug her. The scars inflicted by his father obviously went much deeper than his skin.

"There you are!"

Mel turned, trying not to look guilty for missing curfew. Callie wasn't her mother.

But still.

"Hey. Sorry I didn't call, but…"

"So spill." Her dark eyes sparkled. "How was sex with your Guardian?"

Mel raised a brow, biting back a smile. "Wow. You've had a sudden change of heart."

"Not really." She rolled her eyes. "I'm still honoring the pact, but you seem dead set on breaking it so the least you can do is let me live vicariously through you."

Laughter bubbled up—she couldn't help it. "Without giving you any graphic details, my Guardian rocks in the sack." Mel nodded slowly, her mind replaying the way he put her legs over his shoulders and pulled her down the bed. She cleared her throat. "But there's something else I wanted to talk to you about."

"That's all I get?"

Mel grinned. "Yep."

"Thanks for nothing. Looks like I won't be doing much living through you." She tangled her fingers in the back of her short hair. "What did you need?"

Mel sobered. "Maybe we should go inside. Are the others around?"

"No. Did you want me to make some calls?"

Mel shook her head. "That's good. I was hoping to keep this just between you and me."

Callie dropped her hand to her side. "This isn't about sex with your Guardian?"

Mel chuckled. "I already told you that part of the night was incredible. No need for counseling there. But I do need a little perspective on something else."

"Tease," she grumbled, going back inside the house.

Mel followed her into the den. Callie took a seat behind the desk, and Mel settled in the other chair. "Nate had an abusive, alcoholic father," she told her friend.

"Wow." Callie's expression softened as she got up and came around the desk. "He shared that with you already?"

Mel laced her fingers together, staring at her hands. "He was careful not to let me turn on the light during sex." She lifted her gaze. "I guess I should back up to the part where his partner, Detective Gilman, warned me that Nate isn't a relationship guy."

"That makes sense." Callie nodded. "Physical abuse by a parent when you're a child often makes it difficult for an adult to trust. If he's never been to therapy, then he's probably still keeping others at a distance, protecting himself on some level."

"I gave him the option to take me home last night. You know, *after*. For a second, I thought he'd take it, but then he didn't."

Callie leaned against the edge of her desk. "And then he shared about his father?"

"No." Mel glanced out the window, trying not to see the burns all over his chiseled torso in her head. "I saw all the scars when I woke up this morning, and I asked about them."

"Oh." Callie nearly winced.

"That doesn't look like a good face."

"Well, at least he told you and didn't just pack you up in the car and drive you home." She shook her head slowly. "But if he kept the light off and doesn't usually let dates sleep over, you might be the first woman he's had to confront the scars with."

It wasn't tough to connect the dots. "Shit. You're trying to tell me I may not see him again, aren't you?" Her heart twisted, and in a sick way, her inner muse drank in the pain.

"It's always the worst-case scenario with you." Callie swiped her hand in the air. "I'm not saying he's running, but you might need to give him space. And time to come to you." Her voice softened. "As a child, he had no control and no way to protect himself. Now he's an adult who can be sure he never lets his guard down enough to be hurt again."

"I'm not going to hurt him."

Callie sighed, crossing her feet at the ankles. "Sadly, that has very little to do with it. After one night of sex, he slipped up. He let you stay over and you saw the scars. He opened up more than he intended, and now he's vulnerable. If you push, he'll cut you out of his life. Probably permanently."

Mel huffed out a slow breath, staring at her hands in her lap.

Callie straightened up. "It's the little boy in him making these emotional decisions. You'll have to be patient for the man to come around and realize he's safe with you."

"So texting him to see if I can move in would be a bad idea?"

Callie chuckled. "If you're ready to move in with him after one night, then that really was some incredible sex."

The corner of Mel's lips curved up. "The gods gave me a gift when they marked Nate for me." The smile faded as quickly as it appeared. "But where were they when he needed them most?"

NATE'S HANDS WERE sweating by the time he dropped Mel off at Callie's place, his gut tied in knots. She'd seen the goddamn scars. He shouldn't give a shit. He'd lived. His dad hadn't touched him in twenty years. It should all be behind him.

But somewhere in his sick head, whenever he looked at the damned things, he still heard his father's sloppy voice. *You're nothing. Waste of skin. Nothing.*

One look in the mirror and he was seven years old again.

When he had his shirt on, the little boy was gone. He was Detective Nate Malone and even badass criminals didn't mess with him. So why was he so fucking shaken up about Melanie Jacoby?

Her pep talk about the scars making him a survivor was kind. He got it, but deep down, they were a physical reminder that he couldn't protect himself. Hell, he'd failed Maggie and her mother, too. And now he was supposed to keep Mel safe?

He walked up the cracked cement walk to the yellow-stuccoed home and rapped his knuckles on the door. Mrs. Gaines answered. "Detective Malone! Great to see you."

Her silver hair was pulled back into a clip as she opened the door wider. From the back of the modest tract home, Maggie squealed. Mrs. Gaines, her foster mother, smiled, years of warm laughter lining her eyes. He'd been so lucky to get Maggie placed with her. The first two homes were... Well, he didn't want to think about it.

Nate stepped inside, mustering a smile. "Looking gorgeous today, Mrs. Gaines."

She grinned, swatting his arm playfully. "You're a fine liar."

From his easy chair in front of the football game, Mr. Gaines chuckled. "Someday my bride has to learn to accept an honest compliment."

Maggie raced toward Nate then, slamming against his legs and holding him tightly. He bent to scoop her up, drinking in her giggles. "Ready for mini golf?"

"Yes!" Her gap-toothed grin was a balm to his reopened old wounds. Freckles dusted her cheeks and nose, and her bright-green eyes made it impossible to resist smiling.

"Good." He turned to Mrs. Gaines. "Is it all right if we grab burgers afterward?"

"Sure."

"One less mouth to feed," Mr. Gaines called.

His wife chuffed, swiping her hand in his direction. "Old coot." She patted Maggie's knee. "Have a wonderful time."

Nate pulled into a parking spot at the Family Fun Center and glanced over at his tiny passenger. "I think you're going to be a natural."

Maggie nodded slowly, giving it plenty of thought. "I think I will, too, because Mrs. Bunny says I'm a graceful ballerina with cord-nation."

He struggled to keep a straight face. "Mrs. Bunny is

a smart lady."

"Best ballet teacher ever." Maggie unbuckled her seat belt and opened the booster seat. "Thanks for getting me in dance class, Uncle Nate."

He blinked. He'd asked Mrs. Gaines not to mention that he'd paid for the classes. Over the past two years, he'd fallen for little Maggie, but she deserved a family with a mom and a *loving* dad this time. A single police detective wasn't the stable family life a little girl needed.

He hoped she'd be adopted. But some parts of him, selfish parts, were glad he still got to be her "uncle."

After carefully selecting their colored golf balls, they headed for the first hole. Nate gave Maggie a club and stood behind her, leaning over her tiny frame to show her how to hold the club and gently tap her golf ball. Her first shot bounced off the brick beside the ramp and came right back. She turned her face up to him. "Do I get another chance?"

"All the chances you need."

If only life were like that…

By the third hole, Maggie was getting the hang of it. Mrs. Bunny had been right. The little girl was definitely coordinated. He was careful to miss some putts just to keep the game close, and when she beat him by two strokes, her joy made it all worthwhile.

Maggie bounced around, riding her golf club like a wooden pony. "I did it. I golfed!"

"Yes, you did." He chuckled and collected the

clubs.

"Can we go back to your house for dinner?"

He mussed her hair. "Sure thing, kid."

They got drive-through burgers, and they carried their bounty to his condo. When he unlocked the door, Maggie rushed directly to his fridge and tugged the door open.

"My gummy worms!" She held up the bag, grinning.

He set the fast-food on the table, struggling to hold back a smile. "I told you I wouldn't eat them."

"Yeah, but sometimes adults get hungry." She put her gummy worms beside her burger and sat at the little dining room table. She looked down at the papers spread across the tabletop. "Are you catching bad guys?"

"I'm trying." He moved the DMV list off the table and pulled out a chair. "How's school going?"

She chomped a healthy bite of burger, hummed with glee, and finally answered. "School is good. My teacher is nice."

"You have lots of friends?"

Her cheery expression faltered, and his chest tightened up.

"Not yet," she said softly.

This was her third new school since she lost her mom. He cleared his throat. "You will. Give it time."

She nibbled on a French fry and stared directly into his soul. "Do you have lots of friends?"

Sometimes her simple questions were far from simple. "I have enough."

"Do you take them to min-ature golf, too?"

The image of Mel putting a plastic ball into a dragon's mouth popped in his head. He smirked. "Nope. Just you."

She groaned. "Uncle Nate, you should take them to *fun* things. Then they'll like you."

He chuckled and tweaked her nose playfully. "Is that the secret?"

She grinned and shrugged. "I dunno." She slurped on her straw and set the cup down. "Will you come to my class and talk about your work?"

Her rapid change in subject had him thinking about his muse again. "You'd probably have to ask the teacher."

She sighed and lifted her green eyes up to meet his. "Everyone is bringing a mommy or daddy. My turn is next week."

Oh Christ. "I'd be honored, Maggie," he said before tears filled her eyes. "Just tell me when. I'll be there."

She ran around the table to hug him. He returned the embrace, wishing like hell he could give her more than an hour in front of her class.

If he could go back in time, he would. In a heartbeat.

CHAPTER 10

HE WATCHED HER with binoculars from across the parking lot. Catching the Muse of Astronomy off guard had been simple. Pick a lock, wait for the right moment, and then help her down the stairs.

But now the muses were on alert. Security cameras were being installed around the dilapidated theater, and the Muse of Tragic Poetry had moved in with another partner in Muses Anonymous, Callie, who, judging by the way she seemed to take charge of the group, he was beginning to suspect was the Muse of Epic Poetry.

She'd also spent an evening with Detective Malone. Ben had taken pictures of them leaving the detective's condo. The photos might come in handy later. He couldn't rush his work. Rushing led to sloppiness, and sloppy wasn't going to lead them into the Golden Age of Man.

He'd be patient. Learn her routines and plot his course accordingly.

Her death would be poetic and beautiful, just like she was. He'd see to that.

Melanie Jacoby got into her car and drove away. He

noted the time and tossed his binoculars on the passenger seat to follow her. Soon they'd meet face-to-face. Very soon.

MEL LEFT HER purse in Callie's guestroom and tried not to notice it had been two days since she'd watched Nate drive away. No phone calls, or texts, or drive-bys. Nothing.

And she might've had chocolate for lunch. Nothing but chocolate.

"Enough," she grumbled under her breath. She popped her shoes off and headed out to find Callie. Being alone made it too easy to wallow. Seriously, she'd known this guy for a week, and had only met him because her friend died at the bottom of their steps.

Not exactly the chick flick meet-cute to sweep a girl off her feet.

But she wasn't like other girls. In a twisted way, tragedy was the trail to her heart. And somehow Nate Malone had navigated that path.

And he was already gone.

Callie was on the phone when Mel entered the kitchen. She smiled and waved as she chattered, and Mel picked up an orange and started peeling. She had forty more term papers to read and grade, but she couldn't focus right now. They could wait an hour.

Callie hung up and leaned on the counter beside

her. "The security company finished installing the cameras at the theater. They'll be monitoring them, but they're e-mailing me a link so we can spy remotely, too."

Mel chuckled. "Other than pigeons getting busy, I'm not sure what there will be to spy on. Whoever planted the explosives isn't going to come back. Not now that the police are looking for them."

"You don't know that. They could be desperate."

Mel smirked. "You're the psychologist here. If these wackos are part of a Kronos cult or something, they're probably intelligent, right? Kronos isn't exactly well-known anymore. They'd need to research. And if they think attacking the theater and us will punish Zeus, then they're misguided, but not stupid. It makes sense on paper. But no way would they risk coming back and getting put in jail. They'll try another tactic."

Callie raised her eyebrows and nodded slowly. "Look who's becoming a profiler. I'm impressed."

Mel buffed her nails on her shirt. "I accept tips." She sobered. "Flip side? They succeeded with Nia. I'd assume they'll be gunning for another one of us. If Nate's right and they have a list of the LLC owners, we could all be wearing targets on our backs."

"At least you have a Guardian."

Mel focused on her orange. "Not sure I still do."

Callie sighed. "Still no word?"

"Nope." Mel popped a piece in her mouth. "Giving him space doesn't seem to be working."

Callie came closer and clasped her shoulder. "Don't let that muse take over. You're doing the right thing. He'll get in touch when he's ready. You'll see."

"I shouldn't even care. I've enjoyed an exciting one-night stand before."

"This was more."

"It was to me." Mel pressed her lips together and nodded slowly. "I'm an idiot."

Callie went into the kitchen. "You're not an *idiot*. You're a *romantic*. Big difference."

"Pfft. More like a glutton for punishment."

Callie grinned. "No wonder you're hooked on this detective. You two are probably a match made in heaven."

Mel rolled her eyes. "The gods have a sick sense of humor."

JOHN'S MEETING WITH Belkin Oil had turned up another dead end. No Lewis Gold on payroll. No way to prove they were involved.

Nate rubbed his forehead. "We need to bring the dockworker back in. See if we can get a physical description of this 'Lewis Gold'. He's our only lead right now."

John nodded. "I'll get a sketch artist in with him and see if we can find this guy." He paused. "You okay?"

Nate dropped his hand to the desk. "Yeah." He tipped his chair back, lowering his voice. "I'm visiting Maggie's class tomorrow."

He raised a brow. "What for? Someone picking on her? I thought this was a better school."

"Nothing like that. It's bring-your-parent-to-class month. She asked me if I'd come since…"

"Her dad is in jail."

Nate nodded slowly. "And her mom is dead."

John shook his head. "You were cleared on that whole deal, Malone. Let it go."

He stared up at his partner, and other than Mel, his only friend—if he could even call Mel a friend. "Being cleared of wrongdoing doesn't bring her mother back."

"Neither will going to her class."

"She *can't* be the only one who doesn't have anyone to share. I won't let that happen."

"What about her foster parents?"

Nate sighed. "She asked me, John. How can I tell her no?"

John rubbed his chin. "You're in way too deep on this one."

"I know." He sighed, focusing on his desk. "But I'm all she has left."

Nate finished the paperwork in the stacking file on his desk and left the station. He headed right for the beach. Ever since Mel had slept over at his place, his mind was jumbled, his heart hurt, and he couldn't get her out of his head. He'd lost count of how many times he'd picked up his cell phone to call, but he hadn't done it. He'd told her secrets he never wanted anyone to know, and he had no clue how to get back on level ground with her.

What if she thought less of him now? If there was a trace of pity in her eyes, he'd vomit. So rather than risk it, he'd been trying to push her out of his thoughts.

But his goddamn shoulder burned again. "Fuck it."

He tugged his cell from his pocket and stared at her number. What if she saw his name and ignored the call? He opted for a text. No chance of voice mail, or worse, having her answer with sympathy in her smoky voice.

> *Hey Mel. I'm a hell of a Guardian. You have every right to hate me, but if by some crazy chance you don't…text me back.*

He put the phone away and pulled in a long, slow breath of the ocean air. The waves always gave him a sense of calm, reminded him that his problems were small in comparison. And no matter how hard the waves crashed, they always came back to try again.

His phone buzzed.

He took it out again, and a smile tugged at his lips.

Crazy chance was all it said.

He placed a heavy finger on her name, and the phone rang.

"Long time, no see. Well, not really a long time," Mel said with a small laugh. "Felt long, though."

"Too long." He swallowed the lump in his throat, staring at the water. "Sorry. It's not you, I just…"

"Let's not do this on the phone." Her keys jingled in the background. "I forgot something at school, and I was on my way over to grab it. Want to meet me there?"

"Yeah." He nodded. "I'll be right there."

"Perfect. See you soon." She hung up, and he glanced at the screen.

They talked for less than two minutes, but in that time, he didn't catch a trace of pity or judgment. She was just Mel. And dammit, he missed her. His muse.

He got up from the bench and jogged to his car. There was a dark voice inside him that warned him, shouting for him to cut all ties, telling him he'd stop missing her eventually. But he placated the fear with the promise that this wasn't a relationship. He didn't need her. He was her Guardian. Nothing more.

When he rolled up at the high school and got out of the car, dread crawled up his spine. It was quiet and something seemed…off. He scanned the parking lot. Mel's car was the only other vehicle nearby. Under the faint yellow of the streetlights, everything was washed into a dreamlike monotone.

But nothing moved. Nothing he could see, at least.

He drew his weapon—trusting his gut—and ventured deeper into the shadows of the central open-air lunch area. He made his way down the dimly lit hallways toward Mel's English building. Crystal City

High was an outdoor campus with about twenty structures on the property. Plenty of places to hide.

Did she seriously come down here alone?

Maybe he was overreacting, but his instincts were on high alert. He came around the final corner to the hallway leading to Mel's English class.

Someone was at the other end in a black hooded robe.

"Police. Freeze!" Nate shouted.

The stranger sprinted the other way.

"Dammit." Nate took off after him, but halfway down the hall, Mel opened her door.

"Nate?"

"Stay inside. Lock the door." He didn't look back.

He should've looked.

As he rounded the corner, he caught a glimpse of the robed figure disappearing around the corner of the gymnasium. He pushed his legs harder, praying he was in better shape than the wacko in the robe.

An engine started on the street.

His lungs ached, but the extra dose of adrenaline kicked in. He couldn't outrun a car, but if he got lucky, he could slow it down. He stopped running, lined up his sights, and aimed for the vehicle. Five shots. One connected with glass, two with metal. And then the silver Honda Accord was gone.

"Fuck!" he yelled, holstering his gun. He spun around and almost plowed right into Mel. "What are you doing out here? I told you to lock the door."

"You didn't have backup."

He blinked. "And I still don't. Do you have a weapon?"

Mel held up her phone. "I was ready to call 9-1-1."

"You could have done that from the room."

She crossed her arms. "I wouldn't have known if you needed me to call if I was hiding in my classroom."

He raked his hand through his hair, grinding his teeth to keep from saying something he couldn't take back later. He grabbed her biceps, trying to make her understand. "If something happened to you…"

He let go of her, pacing in a circle. "Jesus, Mel. If you're going to make me believe I'm some kind of Guardian, you have to let me do my job. I can't protect you if you don't listen to me when I tell you to fucking hide."

She put a fist on her hip, jutting it to the side. "You don't know me well yet, so I'm going to give you the benefit of the doubt, but if you seriously expect me to hide while you chase after homicidal lunatics without any backup, then you have sorely underestimated me."

"You don't understand." He shook his head. "Forget it. Let's see if he left anything behind."

She didn't move.

He groaned. "What?"

"I'm waiting for you to help me understand."

He pulled in a slow breath. "I'm not doing this now. Either come with me willingly or I'll pick you up and carry you."

Her jaw dropped. "You're not serious."

"As a hurricane." He took a step toward her, bending his knees in preparation.

"Fine." She walked past him. Fast.

Good. She might be pissed at him, but she was alive.

When he rounded the corner of her building, he stopped. He raised his hand, feeling like a damned idiot, but without a plate number, he had nothing to lose. Except some pride. He rolled his eyes and groaned before finally pressing his hand to the wall.

Light burst through his head. The robed man's face was hidden behind another gold mask of Kronos. Nate struggled to slow his breathing, to search out details before it vanished. The man carried a silver cylinder, and liquid sloshed inside it as he approached Mel's door.

And then it all faded.

Mel rushed over. "Are you okay? Was it a vision?"

He nodded slowly, regaining his equilibrium. "He had a container full of some kind of liquid, but I didn't see it when he ran from me."

"Do you think he dropped it?" She turned on the flashlight app on her phone and started retracing their steps.

"I don't know. It ended before I could see. He saw me and took off." He watched the beam of light on the ground. "Wait. Move it over to your right again."

That direction she followed without question. He

congratulated himself for not pointing it out. "There. Hold it right there." He squatted down and frowned. "It's a thermos."

He pulled out his phone and hit John's number. "Yeah, it's me. I need you out here at the high school with a forensic team. I think Ms. Jacoby was right all along. Someone murdered her roommate, and she's next on the list."

He straightened up, leaving the thermos on the ground. "John will bring gloves. We'll dust for prints and have the contents tested."

Mel heaved a sigh. "Should we wait in my classroom?"

"Sure." He followed her in and left the door propped open so John could find him. "What was so important you had to come to this poorly lit campus alone at night?"

She chuckled. "You make it sound like a bad decision."

He smiled and kept his obviously correct opinion to himself.

She held up two journals. "My term papers were finished, and I started grading the short stories tonight. But I realized two of them must have missed my bag when I was stuffing them in."

Her idea of *important* and his were very different things.

She must've read the confusion on his face because she shook her head. "You're not a writer, are you?

Once you finish something, even a short story, and give it to another person to read, the panic kicks in. A story is like a tiny piece of your soul, and you give it away."

"Okay…" He still didn't see the urgent need to collect the lost journals before morning.

"Some of these kids will be worried all night that their story was stupid or bad or boring, and if I give them a lame excuse like 'I forgot to bring it home,' it'll make that horrible pit of uncertainty last another twenty-four hours. They'll second-guess themselves, and some of them may never risk sharing their writing with anyone again."

He stared at her for a moment, unable to string words together to describe this woman. "You have no regrets, do you?"

"About?"

"Tonight. Coming here."

"No. I'd do it again." She started to smile. "But next time I'll probably bring Callie's croquet mallet."

"Your students are really lucky to have you in their lives." He meant it. Every word. She cared enough about inspiring them to write that she'd come to this campus at night. On her own time. When she knew she was in personal danger.

He didn't like it, but he could damn well respect it.

"I try." Mel lifted her dark eyes to meet his. "These kids are the future. I'd love for some of them to be writers. We need more good stories. Words are magic."

He closed the distance between them and kissed

her, his fingers threading through her hair. She moaned into his mouth, her tongue tangling slowly with his. If magic had a taste, it was Mel.

Sirens blared in the distance. He broke the kiss, a little breathless. "I came here tonight to apologize for not calling."

"Does it come with a caveat that you'll try to communicate better?"

He chuckled. "Yeah."

A car door slammed outside, but she didn't move. "Why?"

"Why what?"

"Why are you willing to communicate better now? What's changed?" Mel took a step back.

He frowned, unsure what to say.

She sighed. "I know I told you it didn't have to be a relationship, that I could just be your muse, but when you backed off…" She brushed her hair back from her face. "It really hurt, and I realized I'm not sure I can do this. If you're going to be more than my Guardian, then I need to know we'll be there for each other." She swallowed and added. "I want all of you."

John stepped through the threshold. "Hey, Malone. Can you show the team the container?"

Nate didn't take his eyes off of Mel. "Be right there." When his partner walked away, he lowered his voice. "I don't know if I have that to give."

She nodded slowly, but the sadness in her eyes made him ache to take his words back. This was exactly why relationships were a bad idea. They only led to pain.

"Thanks for being honest with me." Mel swiped the student journals from the desk. "I'll be more careful in the future. I appreciate you helping me tonight."

And with that she walked out the door. Nate blew out a breath and glared at the empty doorway. That was it? He didn't fucking think so.

He stormed out the door after her, but John intercepted him with the leader of the forensic team. "The container?"

"Yeah." He took them over to the thermos. "Dust for prints before you open it." He grabbed John's arm. "I'll be right back."

His partner sighed. "Let this one go, Malone."

"That would be easier." He glanced down the hallway. "But I can't. Not like this."

"Shit."

"Exactly." Nate jogged down the hall, calling over his shoulder. "I'll be back in a minute."

CHAPTER 11

MEL YANKED OPEN her car door, drying her cheek with one angry swipe and getting in. This wasn't a tragedy. This was cutting her losses. But the muse inside her kept churning her emotions, feeding on it.

They had one hot night together, and he saved her life and her theater. Okay, so Nate also believed her when no one else did.

But he wouldn't be the last, she tried to convince herself as she got into the car. Somehow that thought didn't make her feel any better, though.

A large hand grabbed the top of her door before she could yank it closed. She looked up into Nate's eyes. The yellow lights over the parking lot stole the bright-green color, but they didn't stand a chance of dimming the intensity.

"We're not finished." A muscle in his cheek clenched.

She raised her chin. "I guess we'll just have to disagree on that."

He didn't release his grip on her door. "In a very short amount of time, I have done my best to accept that I don't have skin cancer or a brain tumor. I'm trying to wrap my head around the facts that sometimes I get visions and I'm supposed to be a Guardian chosen by gods. You've got to meet me halfway."

Mel faced forward. If she kept looking into his eyes, it would be too hard to remember this was the same guy who'd slept with her and then tried to walk away. She'd been cavalier thinking she could keep her emotional distance, but the days of his silence made it clear…This was too risky, even for her. It would hurt too much when he left for good.

"I'm sorry. There's no halfway here." She swallowed the lump in her throat and risked lifting her gaze. "I'm saving myself."

He knelt down, eye level with her, his hand still on the door. "Bullshit."

She raised a brow. "Excuse me?"

He shook his head slowly. "This isn't you. This is that voice in your head telling you the worst-case scenario."

"You told me you can't give me what I need…"

"Right now. Tonight." His eyes searched hers. "Mel, I think about you all the time. I want to spend more time with you, I just…" He stared at the lunch tables and benches in the school's courtyard. "I'm going to screw up. This is all new to me." He sighed, looking her way again. "I need time. Give me that."

"And I need you to talk to me."

The corner of his lips quirked into a lopsided smile. "I think I am."

Her heart fluttered. "Thank you."

"For what?"

Mel rested her head back against the seat. "For not letting me drive away." She glanced his way. "I may have overreacted a little."

"It was a little tragic."

Laughter bubbled up as she rolled her eyes. "You think?" She sighed. "For a guy who doesn't believe in relationships, trying to date the Muse of Tragic Poetry is pretty fraught with peril."

He leaned in and kissed her, long and slow. "I can handle some peril."

Her pulse raced. Damn, the man could kiss.

Nate's partner stepped into the lunch area. She nodded in his direction. "Good thing. Looks like some is headed your way."

Nate looked over his shoulder. "Aw shit. I'll call you later?"

"I'd like that." She chuckled and drove away with a smile on her face.

THE POLICE WERE getting too close. Time to tie up some loose ends. He pulled onto the dead-end street and turned off his lights. Outside of the last house, he double-checked the address. Satisfied he had the right one, he tugged on his black leather gloves and picked up the golden mask, drinking in the power and purpose in its soulless black eyes.

Every war had casualties and every goal had obstacles. Dan Barlow, the dockworker he'd paid off, had just landed squarely into the obstacles category.

He scanned the street, studying every car. On the corner by the cross street was a white Ford sedan. Shit. He laid the mask on the passenger seat and started the engine.

As he drove by, his suspicion was confirmed. A man sat on the driver's side, distracted by a laptop. The dockworker must've talked to the detectives. How much had he told them?

Ben turned down the next block. His mission was still attainable, but he'd have to go on foot and enter through the back. He parked the Honda Accord and put the mask over his head. Each time he bore the likeness of Kronos, his confidence in his mission grew.

This was just another step toward the return of the Golden Age of Man. His name would be remembered for generations. Immortality.

He found a house without a fenced-in yard and quietly passed through. Dan Barlow's six-foot chain-link fence slowed him for a moment. He would need a quick retreat. Climbing the fence could leave him vulnerable if he needed to exit in a hurry. Damn.

After a trip back to the car, he returned with wire cutters. He snipped an opening in the fence and silently slid though. Up the back steps, he peered through the window in the back door. No sign of a dog or a kibble bowl on the kitchen floor.

He lifted his robe to slide the clippers into his pocket and take out the wire garrote. Pulling it tight, he drank in the rush of adrenaline. He released one side and reached for the doorknob.

Unlocked. He smiled behind the mask.

With a patient hand, he opened the door, avoiding any creaking. He stepped into the kitchen and closed the door behind him. The knob squeaked, and he froze, holding his breath.

From the other room, Mr. Barlow called out. "I thought you went to bed!"

Sweat beaded on his brow. He didn't move.

"Meredith?"

He waited, but no footsteps sounded. Finally, he ventured farther into the house. Mr. Barlow sat in an easy chair in front of his television, remote in hand as the channels flipped by.

Creeping closer, the Enforcer pulled the wire tighter. The reflection of the gold mask covered the television screen.

"What the hell?"

Without hesitation, he lunged forward, the garrote catching Dan Barlow under the chin. The dockworker struggled, unable to scream as he tugged the wire, cutting through skin and severing arteries.

The body settled into the chair. He quietly removed the garrote, checking the hallway for any sign of a witness. Reassuring silence surrounded him. He inspected his work to be certain Mr. Barlow would never talk to the police again. Satisfied, he went back out the way he'd come.

Inside the car, he used his robe to wipe the wire clean and took off the mask and gloves.

One more stop.

He drove out of the neighborhood with his headlights off, watching the rearview mirror for the unmarked police car.

Nothing.

His hands slipped on the wheel, slick with sweat, his stomach knotted. Killing the muse had been cleaner. Tonight was messy. Nausea rose each time Mr. Barlow's blood-soaked shirt entered his mind, but his belief in the cause kept him moving forward.

Six months ago, he was a realtor, hustling for his next sale. He never dreamed he'd become so much more. Some might say he was a murderer, but he wasn't. Not really. He was a visionary. There was a big difference.

The Order gave him a purpose. They needed him. He could see the big picture, the end result that justified his actions. Empathy stood no chance against his raw determination.

These were not people. They were obstacles.

The end would justify the means. When the Golden Age of Man returned to Earth, the small sacrifices would be forgotten. And his name would live on forever.

He stopped near the edge of the lake and put the Honda Accord in park. After collecting his belongings, he opened the trunk and removed two pieces of a broom handle. He wedged the first between the driver's seat and the gas pedal. The engine roared. He took a deep breath, tightening his grip on the second wooden dowel.

Now or never.

He hit the gearshift, knocking it into drive. The Honda raced for the lake, down the gravel, and finally off the embankment, launching into the air for a few seconds before it smashed into the water. The engine sputtered as the car succumbed to the black depths. He stood watch, a silent sentinel as the final air bubbles floated to the surface.

With the car gone, he scooped up his things and called Ted Belkin.

"It's done. Send a car to the picnic area at Cascade Lake."

He tucked his cell phone in his pocket and made his way toward the tables in the distance. The loose ends were tied.

Melanie Jacoby was next on his list.

NATE STARED AT the lab results, frustration smoldering. They'd identified the liquid in the canister as concentrated sulfuric acid. The crazy guy in the mask had been planning to attack Mel with *acid*. He wanted her to suffer before he killed her.

Nate shoved the printouts away. No fingerprints. No trace evidence. No leads.

Except for the guy from the dock—Dan Barlow. "John, did you track down Barlow yet? We need a physical description of the guy who paid him."

His partner looked up from his paperwork. "He didn't return my call. I'll head over there tomorrow morning. Maybe we can catch him at work." He paused, tapping his pen against the desk, and gave Nate a warning look. "There's no evidence that the C-4 at the theater is connected with the attempted attack on Ms. Jacoby."

"There was a silver car at both place. It can't be a coincidence. It's all we've got right now." He rubbed his forehead, avoiding eye contact. "Mel's involved with the women renovating the theater, and her roommate was, too. It has to be connected. I haven't found the thread yet, but I will."

John leaned back in his chair. "She's under your skin."

Nate raised his gaze. "I've never met anyone like her before. She's tough and tender all at once." He shook his head slowly. "I like being around her." He lowered his voice. "Scares the shit out of me."

John stared at him, and Nate waited for his flippant response. Instead, his partner started to smile. "You really do like this one." He crossed his arms. "I didn't think I'd ever see the day."

"Slow down." Nate lifted his hand off the desk. "It's not serious."

John chuckled. "Like hell it's not." He got up. "I know relationships have never been your thing, and I understand being careful, but one day you'll turn around and find yourself retired and alone, and whatever demons kept you from trusting someone and loving them…" He sighed. "They win. Don't let the demons win, Malone."

His partner headed for the door. "I'm going home. You should, too. We'll meet at the dock at nine tomorrow. We can have a chat with Barlow at work."

"See you then."

Nate's pulse was still elevated even after John had left. It wasn't that Nate wanted to be alone, but caring about someone long term meant being vulnerable. He'd spent his entire life being strong—for himself, his mother, victims and their families—but locked away in the shadows of his heart, the fear that maybe his father was right always festered.

Deep down, what if he was nothing?

Enough.

He stood, tossing his paperwork in the inbox on his desk and walked out. Without realizing it, he took his phone out and called Mel's number. It rang a few times and went to voice mail.

"Hey, Mel. I need to talk to you about the lab results from the container we found outside your classroom. Call me back."

He tucked his phone back in his pocket, but by the time he was inside the car, dread radiated through his shoulders, centralized on the damn birthmark. Was she in danger? His pulse hammered in his ears as he jammed the car in gear and headed over to Callie's place.

He resisted the urge to put the emergency light on top of his car. Barely.

When he turned onto Lothlórien Lane to find Mel's car parked at the curb, everything seemed quiet. But the second he got out, his shoulder began to throb. He closed the door as quietly as he could and drew his weapon. These instincts were new, but he was learning to trust them.

He stepped under the cover of a tree. From the shadows, he scanned each vehicle parked on the street.

All empty.

He slid his gun back into his shoulder holster. Maybe paranoia was infecting him. He started to cross the street toward Callie's house when tires screeched, followed by the sound of scraping metal. He spun around and barely jumped out of the path of a dirt bike. The headlight was off, and the bike skidded on its side on the pavement. The rider jumped free.

"Watch where you're going, man. I almost hit you." The guy stalked past Nate to pick up the motorcycle.

He was dressed head to toe in black, including his helmet. Nate pursued him, putting himself in front of the motorcycle. "This isn't street legal without lights."

The headlight blazed to life, blinding him for a minute. Nate grabbed the handlebar, and a vision burst behind his eyelids. The guy on the dirt bike was on foot, casing the perimeter around Callie's place. His helmet was still on, but the visor was up. He raised night-vision binoculars.

And then it was gone. Nate blinked, tightening his grip on the bike. "You need to get off the motorcycle. Now."

From behind the visor, he said, "I haven't done anything wrong."

"Detective Malone." Nate used his free hand to yank his badge off his belt. He held it up. "Crystal City PD. Get off the bike. I won't ask again."

The engine roared to life. The rider let out the throttle and forced Nate to jump out of the way or be run over.

"Fuck."

Nate ran after him for a few paces, but the taillight faded into the darkness. He didn't even get a partial plate number. Frustrated, he turned back. If he didn't start connecting some of the dots in this case soon, he was going to lose his shit.

He knocked on Callie's door and waited. The door opened, and he looked down to see Mel's friend smile.

"Good to see you, Detective Malone."

"You can call me Nate." He glanced over her—hard not to with their height difference. "Is Mel around?"

She nodded and stepped back to let him pass. "She's in the shower. Want to come in and wait for her?"

"Thanks." He came all the way inside and took a seat on the leather sofa in the living room.

"Would you like something to drink?"

He shook his head. "I'm fine, thanks. Did you notice anything strange tonight, noises or anything?"

"No." Callie frowned. "Why?"

He stared at her, wondering how much Mel had told her about him. Did she know he was a Guardian with a bizarre gift? He kept his game face on. "Just curious. After seeing that guy outside Mel's school last night, I'm a little punchy."

Callie sat down and crossed her ankles. "I'd be worried if you weren't." She smiled. "The gods picked a great Guardian."

He raised a brow. "Mel told you?"

She nodded slowly. "Yeah. Since we lost Nia, we've been circling the wagons. Secrets sink ships."

"I thought it was loose lips."

"Is it?" Callie grinned, mischief in her dark eyes. "Either way, I think she's really fond of you."

He shifted in his seat a little with the uncomfortable turn in the conversation. "Mel's pretty amazing."

"You got that right." She laced her fingers together, hooking her hands on her knee. "So why did you really ask about hearing anything?"

"Nate?"

He turned to find Mel coming down the hall wrapped in nothing but a towel. For a second, his brain disengaged, his body driving him to distraction.

"Are you okay?" she asked, concern in her dark-brown eyes.

He shook it off and struggled to focus. "No. We got the labs back and the stuff he had in the container was concentrated sulfuric acid. Sadly no fingerprints, and I still have no leads on the silver Honda Accord."

Mel frowned. "You think he was going to attack me with acid?"

She came around and sat beside him. The urge to touch her skin was overwhelming. He ground his teeth together fighting to stay on topic.

"It doesn't fit, though. He made Nia's murder look like an accident. Acid would be far from accidental."

Callie cleared her throat. "Since psychology is my field, maybe I could offer some insight?"

Nate glanced her way. "I'm short on leads. I'm willing to take all the help I can get."

"Mel mentioned you think he got our names from our LLC, right? What if he figured out which of the muses we represent?"

The surreal strangeness of discussing muses and Guardians with someone other than Mel made it tough not to let nervous laughter interfere.

"Why would knowing which muse you are make any difference?"

"Well..." Her gaze darted between them, her expression intense and somber. "Nia was inspired by the

Muse of Astronomy. He shoved her down the stairs and left her in darkness. She was all light all the time. What if he knew?"

Mel leaned forward and somehow the towel stayed in place. "So if he knows the Muse of Tragic Poetry is inside me…"

A cold chill ran up Nate's spine. "Scarring your beauty with acid would be tragic."

Mel crossed her arms. "I don't like where this is going."

Nate's gaze locked on Callie. "I'm going to need a list of who's who. Maybe I can get ahead of this guy."

Mel stood. "I'm going to get dressed."

Nate caught her hand before she could walk away. "There was a guy on a motorcycle outside. He was trying to ride off without his headlight. When I grabbed his handlebar I saw him walking the perimeter of this house with night-vision binoculars."

Mel frowned and glanced at Callie. "If he's after me, I'm putting you at risk by staying here."

Callie crossed her arms. "I have an alarm. I'll call the security company tonight and have them install a couple of cameras outside, too."

Mel sighed. "If you're not worried, I'll try not to be, but you know how my head works."

"Worst-case scenario." Callie straightened.

"Yeah, in my head, the man in black comes here for me and we all get murdered." She shook her head with a sarcastic smile. "On that happy note, I better get dressed."

CHAPTER 12

MEL WALKED AWAY and disappeared into a room at the end of the hallway.

Nate faced forward again, keeping his voice low. "I can probably get you both into a safe house until we catch this guy."

Callie squared her shoulders, chin raised in defiance. "This is my house. I'm not leaving."

Nate rolled his eyes. "Mel told me you're the Muse of Epic Poetry, so I'm guessing your impulse is to charge into battles, but that's how people end up dead."

"Many people are dead years before their hearts quit beating." She raised a brow, her dark eyes pinning him to his seat. "Some things are worth rushing into."

He shook his head and stood. "Install the cameras. I'll see about getting a black-and-white to stake out the house for a couple days." He checked down the hall to be sure Mel wasn't nearby. Satisfied, he turned back toward Callie. "I'm not letting someone hurt her on my watch."

"How are you going to accomplish that?" Callie almost smiled. "Are you moving in?"

"Wait a minute," Mel said from behind him. "What

did I miss?"

Nate frowned at Callie. Mel came up beside him, and he took her hand. "No, I'm not moving in, but you should stay with me for a while. And bring some extra clothes."

Mel nudged him. "Ease up, Detective. Stop telling me what to do and explain what's going on."

"Look, you're the one who said I was marked by the gods to be your Guardian." He released her hand, hoping she didn't notice the sweat beading on his palms. His world was tilting on its axis, his gut instinct screaming to back off and protect himself, and his heart insisting that he keep her safe. The conflict warred inside until he struggled to keep his voice even. "We talked about this. Let me do my job."

Callie stood. "I'm going to leave you two alone. If you need me, I'll be in the kitchen."

Once she left, Mel met his eyes. "You're scaring me. Weren't you the one needing time?"

He nodded and rubbed the back of his neck. "I don't know what else to do, Mel."

She tugged his hand. "Come with me."

He followed her to the back bedroom—her bedroom. Her college degree was framed and propped up on the dresser, a group photo of her with the other muses in front of the run-down theater, a picture of her with an older couple he assumed were her parents, and one last photo taken in her classroom. In it, Mel was dressed as Juliet with a blond-haired Romeo.

Nate was taller, tougher, and definitely better looking than Romeo, not that he was comparing. Much.

Mel sat on the edge of the bed. "The acid thing is freaking me out."

"Me, too." He settled beside her. "And I'm sorry if I'm being pushy. If I had some solid leads, I'd be less worried about getting you out of here. We're going to talk to the dockworker again tomorrow, and hopefully we can come up with a physical description of the guy who paid him off. But even that might fizzle out."

"Here's the thing." Her gaze locked on his. "I get that you want to keep me safe, and I appreciate it. I'll admit I'm afraid." She swallowed and took a slow breath, but her eyes never left his. "But if you're thinking I should stay with you at your place just so you can keep an eye on me, I have to object."

Nate frowned, shaking his head. "I don't understand."

"I know you don't." Her lips curved into a sad smile.

What was he missing here?

She took his hand, her fingers lacing with his. "I like you. A lot. And I'm okay with relationships. So if we're in close quarters and I get used to waking up with you every day, I'm going to get attached. And while I'm thinking we might have a future, once you catch the bad guy, you'll have your place back to yourself and I'll be out of there."

Realization dawned on him. She was right. He

would catch this guy, and when he did…what then? Indecision settled on his shoulders. But it wasn't about Mel. Not at all.

Strange.

He brought her hand to his lips, barely managing a whisper. "There was a woman who came to the station to file a restraining order against her abusive husband." He stared at their joined hands and forced the words out. "I was a new detective; thought I was bulletproof. She had a little girl hugging her leg with fear in her eyes, and I assured her that we'd keep her and her mom safe. That *I* would keep them safe."

He cleared his throat, forcing the emotions back into their box. "She and her daughter thanked me. I told her if he came anywhere near either one of them, to call and I'd be there." He shook his head, pain searing his chest. "He found out about the restraining order and came unglued. She called 9-1-1, but the call didn't get to me. There was an error in the transfer—maybe the operator couldn't hear her clearly, I'll never know for sure. The call went to the fire department." He ground his teeth together. "By the time I got there…" He choked up, his voice gravelly with emotion. "I found the little girl lying in a pool of her mother's blood, hugging her, and begging her to wake up."

Mel gripped his hand tighter, her lips brushing his temple. He lifted his head to meet her eyes. Her face was blurred from tears he had no intention of allowing to fall.

"Her husband broke in and hit her twenty-five times in the head with a hammer." He pinched the bridge of his nose. "I gave her my word she'd be safe." He clenched his jaw. "I can't go through that again. I won't."

He looked up at the ceiling, struggling to rein in his emotions. "Your life is more important than any hang-ups I might have about relationships. We'll both have to deal with it."

"What am I supposed to do here?" Mel wiped a tear from her cheek. "Sleeping over at your place just one night had you on edge and ready to run. Now you're asking me to stay until you find this guy. It could be weeks, right?" She rested her hand on his thigh, drawing his gaze to hers. "And what about you, Nate? You matter, too."

She was worried about *him*?

Nate couldn't find his footing. Had he ever mattered to anyone? He wasn't sure how to respond. "I'm not going to lie, I'm probably no picnic to live with, but maybe if we don't call it that…"

Mel sniffled, her lips curved up in the corners. "I could just be hiding out."

"Yeah." He nodded slowly. "I have a pullout couch, and I could sleep in the living room. You can have the bedroom."

"I'm sorry. No." Mel put her hand on his chest, her eyes sparkling. "I have to draw the line there. I should at least get sex out of this deal or this really *would* be a tragedy."

He chuckled. Somehow he'd shared one of his darkest moments, his guilt and shame, and not only did he not sense any judgment from her, but she'd managed to make him smile.

He leaned in to kiss her, murmuring against her lips, "I had good intentions, but there's no way I'd be able to keep my hands off you."

She stole one more slow kiss and met his eyes. "So I'm hiding out with my Guardian."

"And I'm protecting my muse."

Mel grinned. "I'll get my things."

BRYCE PUT THE kickstand down on his bike and walked up to the Belkin Oil building. The guard at the gate was gone, and the backdoor was open, just as he'd been told. He jogged up the flight of stairs and caught the elevator on the second floor, avoiding security at the front lobby.

The elevator door closed, encasing him in silent peace. His heart rate had finally calmed to a regular rhythm. He'd never had a run-in with the police before. The rush of adrenaline and fear made him feel more alive.

He stepped out on the top floor. The light was on at the end of the hall.

Ted Belkin looked up from his desk as he approached. "Bryce… Right on schedule." He gestured to a chair. "Please, take a seat."

He did as he was told. That was part of the reason he'd caught Belkin's eye for a spot on this secret project. Apparently his Enforcer was getting out of line. Bryce was more than ready to step in.

Belkin narrowed his eyes. "What did you find?"

"Melanie Jacoby is staying with Callie O'Connor. Others came and went, but those two are living in the house." He set his helmet down. "There was also a police officer hanging around. Maybe a detective. He wasn't in uniform, but he had a badge."

Belkin shot out of his chair. "Dammit! It's like he sees a damned Bat-Signal when it comes to her." He clenched his fists. "Did he confront you?"

"I had my visor down so he didn't see my face. He flashed a badge and ordered me off the bike, but I got away."

Belkin groaned. "Malone? Was that his name?"

"Yeah, that sounds right."

"Shit." Belkin came around from behind his desk. "Did he get the plate number on the bike?"

Bryce shook his head. "I don't think so. I was out of there full throttle."

"Good. Nice work."

Bryce leaned forward in his chair. "Will I be initiated into the Order soon?"

"Not yet." Belkin's gaze locked on his. "I have a few

more missions for you to accomplish first. Keep following my directions to the letter, and you'll be inducted."

Bryce stood up. "Whatever you need."

Belkin almost smiled. "That's what I like to hear."

MEL TUCKED HER overnight bag inside her larger duffel full of clothes. Since Nia's death, she'd pared down her belongings from a condo, to only a few things in a bedroom, to just enough to fit in a duffel bag for her hideout with a detective who kept his heart in a lock box.

What the hell was happening to her life?

Part of her ached to wallow in it. She could cry for days that Nia was gone. Eventually she'd have to go box up everything in the condo. She was tempted to curl up in a fetal position and accept the tragedy, drown in it.

Her eyes welled with tears, but she blinked them back. Before her eighteenth birthday, she'd been an optimist, eager and ready for her next adventure. But the gods had a different plan, choosing her to carry the spirit of the Muse of Tragic Poetry inside her.

She pulled the zipper closed as Callie came into her room.

"You sure this is a good idea?" she asked.

Mel chuckled, slowly lifting her eyes. "It's a

wretched idea, and you know it."

"Then don't do it." A sad smile spread on Callie's lips. "Stay here. I'm not afraid. I'm having security cameras installed outside."

"This was huge for Nate to invite me to his place." Mel hooked the duffel strap on her shoulder. "If I back out, he may never take this kind of risk again. I can't do that to him."

"Well, shit. You already care about him." Callie sighed. "He has a lifetime of experience keeping people out of his heart. What if that doesn't change?"

"But what if it does?"

Callie raised a brow. "Pretty positive thought for Miss Tragedy."

Mel rolled her eyes. "Or it's the damn muse racing for the inevitable heartbreak." She stared at her friend. "I'm scared, Callie. I do like Nate. A lot. And I'm guessing the more time I spend with him, the more my feelings will probably grow. I'm putting myself right in the crosshairs to unleash some monumental drama, but I can't help it. He has the heart of a lion locked away in there. I just need to find the key."

Callie stepped forward and wrapped her arms around Mel, who returned the embrace as a tear slipped from the corner of her eye.

"Tragedy aside," Callie whispered, "he is one lucky son of a bitch." She pulled back to meet her eyes. "And if he hurts you, there is a good chance I'll have to kick his ass."

Mel laughed, staring down at Callie. "Nate was right. You are a firecracker. He's a good judge of character."

Callie grinned. "If so, then he knows the gods blessed him when they marked him for you."

They both turned as Nate filled the doorway. "Didn't mean to interrupt, but we should get going."

Mel walked to his side, and he took the duffel from her shoulder.

She smiled. "You don't need to do that."

"I know." He turned to go to the car.

Callie caught her arm before she could do the same. "Call me later."

Mel nodded. "I will."

THE DRIVE FROM Callie's to Nate's place was spent in awkward silence. Once he parked, Mel forced herself to say what kept playing through her head. "Are you already regretting inviting me here?"

Nate glanced her way, and her heart clenched. His lips gradually curved into a smile she was quickly getting addicted to seeing. "No. But I definitely don't know what to say."

"We could start with what time you need to be up in the morning?"

"John and I are meeting at the docks at nine o'clock. You?"

"I have to be at school by seven thirty." Mel chuckled. "Tragic."

"That is tragic." Nate laughed and took her hand, his touch settling all her jumbled nerves. "We better get you inside."

She got out and followed him to his condo. He carried all her things while she held the keys. After she opened the door, Nate's phone buzzed. He set her bag down and answered.

"Malone." He paused. "Shit. Okay, I'll meet you there."

Nate dropped his phone in his pocket, his smile now a tight grimace. What the hell was he going to do now? "Our only lead is literally dead."

Her eyes widened. "What?"

He raked a hand through his hair. Struggling to keep his cool. "The guy from the dock, Dan Barlow? His wife just found his body. I've gotta meet John at the scene."

"Okay." Her voice was steady, but he couldn't miss the fear in her eyes. "You go. I'll get settled."

Sometimes he forgot that most people didn't deal with murders as often as he did. He took her hand, his gaze locked on hers. "No one except Callie knows you're here. Keep the door locked and your phone handy. Call me even if you think it's nothing."

She nodded. "I'll be fine." He couldn't tell if she was trying to convince him or herself. She squeezed his hand. "Go. Get these bastards."

He leaned down to kiss her cheek. "I'll be back as soon as I can."

Nate closed the door behind him. Never in his life had he wanted to come home. He tried not to analyze it, but he smiled as he jogged to the car.

John met Nate at the car as he pulled up to the scene. "Our man was staking out the street all night," John told him. "He didn't see anyone approach the house."

Nate scanned the fence line. "He had to have come through the back. Any prints?"

"They're still collecting forensics, but no prints yet."

"Fuck." He met John's eyes. "His wife didn't hear anything?"

"No." John stepped out of the way of a tech. "She was sleeping with her C-Pap machine humming, and he was in his chair watching TV. She woke up to go to the bathroom and realized he wasn't in bed."

"She's not a suspect?"

"I doubt it." John shook his head. "His throat was cut, and she doesn't have any blood on her or any trail that could lead to a stashed weapon. She's pretty upset. We'll see if there's any evidence linking her, but it doesn't look likely."

Nate headed for the front door with John right behind him. The medical examiner was already on the scene investigating the victim's body. The television was still on.

He approached Barlow's wife and knelt by her side where she sat in a dining room chair, hair rumpled in mismatched sweats. "I'm sorry for your loss, Mrs. Barlow."

She sniffled and met his gaze. "Dan was a good man."

Until he took money from the wrong guy. "I need to ask you a few more questions so we can find the person who did this."

She nodded and wiped her nose.

"You said you didn't hear a struggle. Did you notice any noises out back?"

"Nothing. I have sleep apnea. The doctor gave me a machine to help me sleep. It blows air. I didn't hear anything." She rocked slowly in her chair. "I work early in the morning so I was in bed by nine o'clock. Who would do this?"

He didn't know for sure yet, but he had a strong hunch it was a man wearing a gold mask of Kronos. "We're going to do our best to find out. Is there anyone we can call for you?"

"I already called my sister. She'll be here soon."

"Did your husband have any enemies that you know of?"

"No." She shook her head. "Everyone liked Dan."

He handed her his card. "Call me if you remember anything else, okay?"

"Thank you." She took the card.

Nate got up and stood beside his partner. "Can you watch over things here? I'm going to take a look out back."

He took a flashlight from one of the techs and pulled on a pair of latex gloves. If he stumbled onto anything that might have fingerprints, he didn't want to chance contaminating the evidence. He nodded to his partner and headed out the back door.

The cool night air settled over him as he swung the flashlight slowly from side to side, searching for any sign of blood or an entry point to the property. He'd have to walk the fence line to search for openings, but he was grateful to be doing it alone. His gut told him this was all connected, and if he had a vision, he didn't want an audience.

About ten feet from the back steps, he noticed a drop of blood. He pulled an evidence flag from his pocket and stuck it in the ground to mark the spot. It was probably from the victim, but the forensics team might be able to find trace elements from the weapon, or maybe the killer nicked himself.

Wishful thinking.

Either way, it proved his theory that the attacker came through the back. The chain-link fence was eight feet high. A murderer wouldn't risk getting caught or leaving evidence behind from a climb. There had to be an opening in the fence someplace.

He tucked the flashlight under his arm and braced

himself before he touched the fence. Nothing. Nate frowned. Then he remembered the gloves. He pulled off the latex and tried again.

A movie came to life in his head. The man in the black robe and gold mask; he clipped the chain-link on the back fence line.

And before going through, he removed the mask.

Nate's heart rate double-timed. Straining, he struggled to make out the killer's face, but the shadows kept it hidden. He had short brown hair, no earring, no tattoos that he could see, and in his other hand, two wooden handles hung down from a wire.

Then Nate was alone in the backyard again.

Nate pulled the glove back on, blinking until his vision cleared. He had to find the opening. Maybe the robe got snagged or the gold was scraped off the mask. He was stretching, but he needed something.

He had to get this guy and keep Mel safe.

When he found the opening, he removed the glove again. Nothing. Shit. He tucked the glove in his pocket and slid through. Sweeping the beam of light back and forth, he marked another drop of blood.

And then the trail was gone.

"Dammit."

He turned to go back to the crime scene, formulating a way to let them know the murder weapon was a garrote without mentioning a vision.

CHAPTER 13

Mel shoved Nate's clothes over in the closet and managed to squeeze hers in beside them. His scent was everywhere, intoxicating her. Suddenly, finding a place to put her things away had become more intimate than she'd intended.

With that finished, she wandered into the little kitchen. If she was going to be here for a few days, they'd need food in the fridge. She opened the door, her gaze immediately dropping to the bottom shelf. The gummy worms were gone.

She smiled imagining her big strong Guardian munching on them while he worked. Shaking her head, she went about making a mental grocery list. It was easier to note the items he did have rather than figuring out what she needed to buy. She started opening kitchen drawers in search of a pen and paper. Instead, she found a drawing—a little girl with a big man drawn in felt-tip marker.

In spite of being stick people, the man had green eyes and a badge on his belt. At the bottom someone had scrawled "Thank you!" followed by hearts and happy faces.

She flipped it over, but there were no markings or dates. Nate told her he never had a relationship, but could he have a daughter? One wild night with an accidental conception? From the stick people, she couldn't tell if there was a resemblance.

There had to be some other explanation. He would've told her if he had a daughter.

Or at least she thought he would… But when? Before or after they had sex?

Other than being a police detective with an abusive, alcoholic father, she didn't know much about the man she was now sharing a closet with.

She put the picture back in the drawer and kept looking for paper. She finally found one, as well as colored pens and Post-it notes. Good enough. Once she had her list of essentials, she glanced at the clock. It was after one in the morning. She had to be up for school in a few hours. She left the list on the counter and fired off a quick text to Nate.

> *Early day for me so I'm going to get some sleep. Will you be back soon?*

As soon as she hit "Send," regret swelled. Why had she asked when he'd get back? This wasn't supposed to be a relationship. This was her hiding and him protecting; possibly with bedroom benefits on the side.

Before she could build her angst into a full-blown panic, he texted back.

Sorry it's so late. I'll be there in an hour max.

Two sentences, but she managed to read enough subtext into them to make her head spin. Was he sorry she was still awake, sorry she was at his place, or sorry he ever met her? She set her phone aside and headed to the bedroom to change. When she came back to the sofa, she was in one of Nate's T-shirts. At this point she figured she'd just wait up for him. But her body seemed to have a different plan.

Nate's front door was locked. Good. Mel was being safe. The second he opened the door, an unusual swell of emotion overcame him. He smiled, closing the door quietly behind him, as he saw she was passed out on the sofa, curled up in one of his shirts.

Seeing her calmed him, and in the same moment, it watered the seed of worry germinating inside his heart. He didn't want to like having her here. It wasn't Mel. She was amazing. But the idea that he might get used to the company, to that warm feeling of finding her sound asleep in his T-shirt? It was a dangerous path. It led to caring and depending, and ended in pain.

He went back to his room and turned on the closet light. His clothes were moved and hers added. His pulse sputtered. It was stupid to let it bother him. She had to put her clothes someplace. And he was the one who'd insisted on keeping her safe.

And dangerously close.

He forced himself to move. Obsessing over her moving in was going to drive him out of his mind. On the shelves at the back of the closet, he took down a blanket, turned out the light, and brought it out to cover her.

She hummed and opened drowsy eyes. "You made it back."

He sat on the edge of the couch beside her. "I didn't mean to wake you."

She leaned up and rested her head on his shoulder. "Sorry I texted you. I guess I was worried or something."

He lifted her chin. "I work crappy hours."

"I wasn't trying to make it seem like…"

"Like you cared?"

She chuckled. "I do care, but I didn't want to suffocate you with it. You don't owe me anything."

He kissed her forehead. "This is hard for me, too."

"Any leads?"

He shook his head, unwilling to let the frustration creep back in. He turned and scooped her into his arms, lifting her up as he stood. Mel gasped, then wrapped her arms around his neck. "Not interested in talking about work?"

He claimed her lips, savoring the taste of her as he carried her into his bedroom. Laying her on the bed, he settled over her. "Work fell off my radar the second I walked in the door."

The corner of her mouth lifted into a crooked smile. "Me in your shirt works for you."

"*You* work for me." He kissed her again, hard this time.

Her lips parted, his tongue swirling with hers. Usually a rough night of work meant a long night of push-ups and sit-ups in the hope that exhaustion would lead to sleep. Mel's fingers tightened in his hair, her other hand sliding down his back.

She beat the hell out of exercising.

His voice became a growly whisper. "I need to get out of these clothes."

He stood up and started to unbutton his shirt when the lamp clicked on. He frowned. "Something wrong?"

"Nope." Mel stared up at him, the T-shirt barely covering her. His erection pulsed, and she wet her lips. "Just wanted to watch."

He fumbled with the next button and shook his head. "I'm better with the light off."

"You know how you like seeing me in your shirt?" She pulled it off and dropped it over the edge of the bed. "Now you can see me without it."

He drank in her naked body, his fingers suddenly making fast work of his buttons. He hesitated before taking it off completely. "You're so sexy."

Her eyes sparkled. "So are you."

She'd already seen his scars and accepted him. He had nothing left to hide. But his heart still raced as he opened his shirt and took it off. Her lips parted slightly in answer. Seeing the desire on her face, her body… Damn, it made him even hotter.

He brought his hands to his slacks and unbuckled his belt. She swallowed, her breath catching. He came closer to the bed, running his hand up her leg. "I've never wanted anyone this bad before."

"Good." Her fingertips slid up the length of his zipper, squeezing his erection until he ached for her touch. She sat up and unfastened the button. Looking up at him from under her thick lashes, she reached for his zipper. "I want you, too."

She eased his zipper down and tugged his pants over his hips until he was finally free. He stared down at her as she took him into her mouth. The sight of her lips sliding down his shaft nearly did him in. He ground his teeth, struggling to keep control, to make it last. Tangling his fingers in her hair, he rocked into her mouth slowly.

Her fingernails slid up the back of his legs, teasing his ass, encouraging him as she sucked gently. He growled her name. Every muscle in his body tensed. Too close. He didn't want it to be over yet. "No more. I'm about to lose it."

She kissed her way up his bare chest, her wet lips teasing his nipple until she stood before him. He claimed her mouth and bent his knees. Catching her waist in one arm, he straightened, lifting her off the floor. She wrapped her legs around him as he slid his hands along her thighs.

His erection brushed her opening, hot and wet. She rocked her hips, and he sank into her. He groaned into the kiss, his pulse hammering in his ears. If it were humanly possible, he'd never stop making love to her. Never.

MEL COULDN'T CATCH her breath. She broke the kiss, her lips trailing down his neck. In the mirrored closet door, their reflection made her heart race. His muscles were taut, defined, and all hers—at least for right now.

She tingled all over as she nibbled at his ear. "You're so sexy," she whispered.

He turned to kiss her lips and caught their reflection in the mirror. She followed his gaze. He paused, and for a second, she worried everything might be ruined. She clenched her inner muscles and slowly writhed, taking him even deeper. He dropped his head back, thrusting his hips, as his grip on her thighs tightened.

She pulled her attention from the mirror to Nate's face. Sweat glistened on his forehead, and desire burned in his eyes. He kissed her, then growled against her lips, "Come with me."

His hands were busy holding her up, so she brought one hand between them, rubbing with each thrust. He slammed into her harder and faster, and her entire body tightened. She cried out against his shoulder as he erupted deep inside her.

"Mel…" His arms trembled as he walked her to the bed, but his hold on her never faltered. He laid her on the bed, keeping her close so their bodies remained connected. He kissed her shoulder and whispered, "I…" He lifted his head with a crooked smile that made her heart flutter. "No words."

She nodded slowly. "I know what you mean."

He cupped her cheek. "I like being able to see you."

She swallowed the lump in her throat, running her hands up his muscular biceps to his shoulders. "Seeing you…turned me on, too." She shook her head, her lips curving. "You are beyond hot."

He chuckled, rolling his eyes. "I don't know about…" His voice trailed off, his expression sobering. He met her eyes. "Oh shit. I got so caught up…"

Mel blinked. "Condom." She cringed. "Crap."

"Yeah." He slid free from her and sat up. "I'm sorry. Dammit. I've never forgotten before." He looked over at her. "What do we do?"

Her big, strong police detective was asking *her* what to do. She sat up, sliding her arms around his waist from behind him. "We make sure we don't screw up again. It usually takes more than one time to get pregnant." Who was she trying to convince, him or herself? She started doing the mental calculations in her head and breathed a sigh of relief. "I don't think I'd be ovulating yet anyway."

His body tensed up, and a fit of inappropriate giggles hit her. He tried to look back over his shoulder, but she dodged his stare, making the laughter even worse.

"I'm sorry. I guess talking ovulation isn't great pillow talk."

He heaved a sigh and chuckled. "Not a word I use often around here."

"Now I want to get a puppy and name her Ovulation."

He turned around and pinned her on the bed, catching her hands in his. A playful grin she'd never seen before lit up his face. "No puppies."

She mustered her best innocent smile. "Maybe a kitten? We could call her Ovie for short."

He laughed, kissing her long and slow. Her entire body warmed. When he pulled back, his eyes searched hers. For what, she couldn't even venture a guess.

Finally, he whispered, "I'm going to keep you safe."

"I know."

But would he still be there when the threat was gone? She pushed the thought from her mind and got under the covers. *One day at a time.* He held her close, and she drifted off to the steady beat of her Guardian's heart.

HER CELL PHONE buzzed. She squinted, stretching to

turn off her alarm. It wasn't even light out yet.

The joys of teaching...

She eased out from under Nate's arm and got showered and dressed. Her legs were sore, but she smiled remembering the amazing workout she'd gotten the night before.

Yeah, it was going to be a good day.

She waited for her inner muse to cast a shadow over it or remind her that she could be pregnant, but there was no sign of tragedy.

Once she was ready, she came into the bedroom and found Nate awake. She frowned. "Sorry. I didn't mean to wake you."

"How are you feeling?"

She started to smile. "Really good..." He looked concerned. A light bulb came to life over her head. "And definitely not feeling pregnant."

The corner of his lips curved. "Probably too soon anyway, right?"

She nodded. "Way too soon." Before she could stop herself, the words fell from her mouth. "Do you have any children?"

He grimaced a little and raised a brow. "I told you this is the first time I ever forgot a condom. And I've never been married."

"Right." Heat flushed in her cheeks. "I just... I was looking for a piece of paper yesterday and saw a drawing of you and a little girl. I just assumed..." She shook her head. "I better get to work. See you later."

She scooted out before things could get any more awkward. And somewhere deep inside, her inner muse reveled in it.

NATE WAITED FOR the door to close before he sat up. He hadn't meant to keep Maggie a secret, but he'd also been hoping to protect Mel without having to share everything.

Old habits die hard. Part of him was still bracing for the fall out, protecting himself. *Oh shit. Maggie.*

He had to go talk to her class.

Pulling up the calendar on his phone, he double-checked the time. Three o'clock. Then he was going to take her to get some ice cream. He fired off a text to Mel.

> *The little girl's name is Maggie. She's not mine, but she's pretty amazing. I'm supposed to speak to her class at 3.*

He hit "Send" and stared at his phone. His palms started sweating. He was getting in too deep, but it was so easy where Mel was concerned. Screw it.

> *Want to come?*

He set the phone down and went to the closet. Before he had his shirt buttoned, his phone chimed. He picked it up and smiled.

I'm off at 2. Pick me up?

He shouldn't have been so eager, but he texted back immediately.

See you then.

What the hell was he doing?

CHAPTER 14

"Y OU'RE IN A good mood for a guy who lost his only lead last night." John dropped off a Styrofoam cup of coffee on Nate's desk. "What's up with you?"

Mel's face filled his head. He picked up the coffee and grinned. "Nothing. I figure the murder tells us I was right about everything being connected. We were getting too close."

"And now we're miles away again."

"Nah. Belkin Oil is involved. I don't know exactly how yet, but I'm going to find out."

"Without a murder weapon and a suspect, it'll be tough to make anything stick," John said. "Belkin will have the ultimate legal team, too, I'm sure."

"That's why we need more evidence." Nate sipped his coffee. "And we've got to find Lewis Gold."

"If he exists."

"He can't hide forever." Nate finished his coffee and dropped the cup in the trash. "I've gotta leave at two today."

John crossed his arms. "Hot date?"

Nate shook his head slowly. "Maggie."

John sighed. "Not sure if that's better or worse. You're still hoping she gets adopted, right?"

"Just cover for me, okay?"

He nodded. "You know I will."

"Thanks, man."

Nate worked through his lunch hour, eating a sandwich at his desk, trying not to keep checking the clock. Not that he was eager to see Mel. He just didn't want to be late to Maggie's school. Mostly.

When he got to Mel's high school later, the parking lot was busy. The fact that many of the drivers had only been behind the wheel for a year or less also made it hazardous. But he only used the horn once.

Two students were still at Mel's desk when he walked through the door. The girl looked up at him and then quickly away, her cheeks coloring. But the boy tipped his head. "This your new man, Ms. Jacoby?"

Mel chuckled. "Brian, this is *Detective Malone*."

Brian did a good job covering that he just swallowed his gum. Nate slid his sunglasses down a little so the kid could see his eyes. "Good to meet you, Brian."

Brian grabbed the girl's hand. "Come on, Carla. We gotta get to Chem Lab."

Mel called after them. "Don't forget to practice your poems for the slam tomorrow."

Brian waved over his head as he and the girl crossed the threshold.

Nate grinned as he approached her desk. "I'm almost sorry I'll be missing your slam poetry tomorrow."

She rolled her eyes, but her smile was still addictive. "You are not." She grabbed her bag and a flash drive, then straightened up. "So tell me about your presentation. Which grade is Maggie in?"

"Second grade." He offered her his arm, ignoring the flush of electricity coursing through him from the simple touch. "I'll be talking about being a detective to a bunch of seven-year-olds. Now you see why I wanted some backup?"

Mel laughed and squeezed his bicep. "And how did you get roped into this?"

He opened the car door for her and came around to his side. Once he was inside, he turned the key and glanced her way. "Maggie was the little girl I told you about, the one who lost her mom to her abusive father."

Mel's smile faded. "Oh... Did you arrest her dad?"

"Yeah." He lowered his voice. "I was the lead detective on the case and testified in court to put him away for life." He met her eyes, but again, there was no sign of judgment there. "She didn't like me much at the beginning. I was the villain, not her dad." He ground his teeth and tightened his grip on the wheel. "But now, other than her new foster parents, I'm all Maggie has left."

Mel's eyes brimmed with tears, but she blinked them away. "This must be Bring Your Parent to School Day?"

He nodded slowly. "She's at a new school. I can't let

her be the only one who doesn't have a parent come."

She rested her hand on his thigh, squeezing it. "You're a good man, Nate Malone."

Hearing her say those words meant more to him than he could articulate. He cleared his throat and pulled into the flow of inexperienced drivers.

"She's a great little girl." He clenched his jaw keeping his eyes on the road. "She got dealt a tough deck of cards. She deserves better."

Mel had never met a man like Nate. He'd been raised by a bastard who made him feel ashamed and unworthy, but instead of being bitter, he did his best to protect others from his own fate. He would probably deny it, but she saw the way he loved others—Maggie and his partner—with tenacity and compassion. But he wouldn't allow himself to commit to it, to really jump in with both feet. At least not when it came to her.

Sadly for her, she was already slipping in.

And she'd been glowing all day. Today, teachers and students alike commented on her smile, her skin, her hair, all without realizing the only thing that had changed was that she'd woken up in Nate's arms.

Hearing about his loyalty to this little girl who had lost so much, only made her feel like she was falling faster. And without a safety net. She hadn't admitted it out loud to another soul, but there was no denying it would be so easy to love Nate Malone.

He pulled to the curb in front of the elementary school and turned off the engine. "Thanks for coming with me today. I…" He stared at the dashboard. "I think Maggie will love you."

Hearing him say the word set off a million butterflies in her stomach. Oh shit. Maybe she was further gone than she wanted to admit.

"Thanks for inviting me along," she said.

She got out and walked into the office with him. When he approached the desk, the receptionist grinned up at him and played with her hair. "May I help you?"

Mel smiled watching the flirtation unfold. Nate saw his scars, but women saw a chiseled detective with eyes that could melt you where you stood.

"I'm here for Maggie Keen."

The receptionist finally noticed Mel and toned down her smile a notch. "You must be her parents. Are you here to tell the class about your job?"

He didn't bother to respond to the first part. "Yes. Do we need badges?"

She pointed to a clipboard. "Sign in here, please. Both of you."

While they filled out the sheet, the receptionist wrote up two stickers that read MAGGIE KEEN. She offered one to each of them. "Put these on. She's in room twenty—down the hallway and to the right."

They stuck the badges on their shirts and headed

for the classroom. Nate stopped outside the door. "Can you wait out here for a second?"

Mel nodded; worried she'd made a bad decision agreeing to come along.

He squeezed her hand. "I'll be right back."

True to his word, he came back, a little girl with a head of strawberry-blonde curls in tow. She gazed up at Mel but didn't say anything. Nate cleared his throat. "Maggie, this is Mel. I invited her to come with me today so she could meet you."

Mel knelt down, eye level with the girl, and held out her hand. "Great to meet you, Maggie."

The little one looked up at Nate and back to Mel. She finally took her hand. "Mel is a boy's name."

Mel chuckled. "It's really Melanie, but my friends call me Mel."

"Maybe we can be friends…?" Maggie's voice was still tentative.

"I'd like that." Mel resisted the urge to hug this little girl who had seen too much tragedy in her few years. "I saw your artwork at Nate's house. You draw much better than I do."

Maggie flashed a smile, and the gap-toothed joy made Mel grin. "Thanks. I like drawing."

"Do you mind if I come in while Nate talks?"

Maggie's eyes sparkled. "You can sit with me."

Mel straightened, her gaze locking on Nate's. He smiled at her, but it was somehow different. Tender? She swallowed hard.

Maggie let go of Nate and took Mel's hand instead. "Come on. I'll show you my desk."

Nate mouthed *Thank you* as she passed by with Maggie, and he followed them inside.

The teacher stood behind her desk. "Okay, everyone, come find a seat on the carpet up here. Maggie has brought her…"

"Uncle Nate," Maggie announced formally. "He's a police detective."

The class came to life, racing to the carpet. Maggie tugged Mel after her. They found a spot, but Mel noticed that none of the other kids sat near them. As a teacher herself, it was easy to read their behavior. Maggie didn't have any real friends here.

Nate started talking, and all the chatter faded away. He told them about his job helping people and solving crimes. He never pulled his gun free of the holster, but he did take off his badge and let the kids pass it around. When he asked for questions, anxious hands popped up.

He answered the first few, everything from have you shot anyone to does your car have lights on it. Finally, he called on a boy near the back of the carpet.

He looked over at Maggie, his eyes narrowing as he smiled and faced Nate again. "Why didn't Maggie's *dad* come to talk to us?"

SHIT. BEFORE NATE could come up with an answer that didn't include her dad being in prison, Mel leaned forward, staring down the kid. "Maggie's got so many people who love her that when her dad couldn't come, we all arm wrestled to see who would get to come to her class. Uncle Nate won."

The class giggled, tension released, and best of all, Maggie grinned. Mel was a damn miracle.

The bell rang, and the kids raced to collect backpacks and homework. He walked over and offered Mel a hand. He pulled her to her feet. "You were amazing. Thanks."

She shook her head. "I work with kids. I'm used to shutting down the ones who think they're better than everyone else. Sad to see it starts so early."

He nodded, keeping an eye on Maggie. "I had to call in a couple favors to get her into this school. She's only been here a few weeks."

"Time to have a barbeque at the park and invite some nice kids," Mel said.

He raised a brow. "It's not her birthday."

"You don't have to wait for a birthday to make some new friends." She chuckled.

Maggie ran over with her FBI Training Academy backpack on her shoulders. "Thanks for coming to my class, Uncle Nate!"

"I wouldn't have missed it." He scooped her up, making her squeal with giggles. "Ready for ice cream?"

"Yes!" He set her down, and she grinned up at Mel.

"Will you come with us, Mel?"

"I'd love to."

Maggie raced ahead of them, and Nate caught Mel's hand, his fingers lacing with hers. She smiled up at him. "Thanks for introducing me. Maggie's a sweet kid."

Maggie babbled about school and the teacher all the way to the ice cream shop. When they got out, she raced up to grab Nate's hand, and then reached her other hand out to Mel. Their three joined shadows stretched out in front of them, making Nate's chest ache. This was the shadow of a family.

One he never had.

One Maggie was missing.

He looked over at Mel. Her attention was on Maggie while they talked about their favorite ice cream flavors. Could life ever be this simple and safe?

Inside, they each ordered a cone and savored their desserts. Maggie's lips were outlined in Rocky Road as she glanced between him and Mel. She tilted her head at Mel. "Are you in love with Uncle Nate?"

He almost choked. Mel nudged him under the table and smiled at Maggie. "Why do you ask?"

"Because he's good and he's lonely. He needs someone to love him."

He should've seen this coming. Why had he thought bringing Mel would be a good idea?

Before he could save himself, Maggie went on. "He should take you to min-ature golf. I told him he has to do fun things to have friends."

Mel grinned. "Speaking of fun things, I was telling Nate it might be a blast to have a barbeque at the park, and you could invite some kids from your class. Maybe make some friends of your own."

Maggie bounced in her chair. "Could we have a piñata?"

Mel nodded. "And we'll stuff it with candy."

While Maggie and Mel plotted, he sat back in awe of this woman who'd completely detoured Maggie's inquisition. His muse was pure magic.

And the more he cared about her, the more his blood pressure rose. She'd given him nothing to fear, but the urge to run raised its ugly head anyway. He would never be worthy of someone like her. She'd realize it eventually. He should save himself while he still had a chance.

He finished his cone and cleared his throat. "We should probably get you back to the Gaineses' house so you can get your homework done."

"Can I come to your house? Mel's a teacher. She could prob-ly help me. Mrs. Gaines says our 'new' math is impossible."

Mel chuckled and rested her hand on Maggie's shoulder. "I'm an English teacher. I'm useless when it comes to math homework, but I promise we'll get the barbeque planning started and bring you invitations for your classmates soon, okay?"

"Okay." Maggie didn't sound excited, but at least

she didn't complain about going back to her foster home.

When they got out of the car, Mrs. Gaines opened the door and waved. Maggie hugged Nate tightly around the neck and whispered against his ear. "Take Mel to golf. She likes you."

He laughed. "I'll see what I can do."

She pulled back and met his eyes. "See you soon."

Maggie squeezed Mel in a fast hug and then raced up the walkway and into the house.

Mel smiled up at him. "Let me guess, you got her the FBI backpack."

"You saw the way she grilled us at the ice cream shop. She'll be an excellent agent someday."

They got back in the car, and Mel rested her hand on his thigh. "I hope you don't mind the barbeque. It wasn't my place, I know. It's not like we're a couple and Maggie's not our little girl. I didn't mean to overstep my bounds. I just want to see her make some friends at her new school."

He leaned over and kissed her. She moaned, opening her mouth as his tongue brushed her lips. He slid a hand into her hair, wishing he could say the words brewing inside him and praying she'd feel them.

Then her cell phone chimed. Horrible timing.

She pulled back, desire in her eyes. "Damned phone." She checked it and frowned. "E-mail from Callie. She needs me at the theater."

"What happened?"

Mel shrugged. "She doesn't say. Just says that it's urgent." She glanced his way. "I know you've got stuff to take care of. If you can drop me back at school, I'll take my car over."

His birthmark started warming with a dull throb. "I should go with you. Just in case."

She frowned. "She didn't say it was dangerous. She probably wants to show me how to set the new security cameras or something. With Callie everything is larger than life and urgent."

"No." The throbbing intensified. "Something's wrong."

Nate turned the car around and raced in the direction of the theater.

He stayed in the shadows of the wings of the theater with his gear. Getting in had been trickier since the muses had installed cameras, but nothing a little black spray paint couldn't fix. He blackened two of the cameras, hacked into Callie O'Connor's e-mail, and now he waited for a response.

Finally, an e-mail popped in his phone saying that Melanie Jacoby was on her way. Perfect.

He checked the pressure on the sprayer, his nerves on high alert. When the acid ambush hadn't worked, he'd decided on a less artistic end for the Muse of Tragic Poetry. He'd douse her in gasoline and set her on fire. He'd cross another muse off the list and burn down the theater all in one evening.

And if the fucking detective was with her, then so be it. He'd kill him, too.

Killing an officer would bring backlash from law enforcement, but he was beyond caring. The detective had a sixth sense when it came to Melanie Jacoby's safety; swooping in to save her at the condo after finding her dead roommate, having the bomb squad defuse the C-4 explosives, and then intercepting him before the sulfuric acid could be put to use.

A car pulled up outside. He reached for his gold mask and put it on. He tightened his hold on the spray trigger.

Glory was only a moment away.

CHAPTER 15

By the time he parked the car, Nate's birthmark was aching, burning. There was definitely danger up ahead.

He drew his weapon. "Wait here."

Mel got out and slammed the door. "You're not going in there without backup."

Dammit. He glanced her way. "It's my job. Get in the car so I know you're safe."

"You call John and wait for him to get here so I know *you're* safe."

"This isn't a game, Mel." He tipped his head toward the car. "I can handle this."

"I'm sure you can, but you're right that this isn't a game. Either you take me as your backup or you wait."

He tightened his grip on his Glock. "We've already had this discussion. Why are you fighting me on this?"

"Because sometimes I think *I* care more about your welfare than you do."

The burning on his shoulder moved to his chest. Had anyone other than his partner ever cared about his welfare?

He clenched his jaw. *Focus, Malone.*

"Fine. Stay behind me, and when I say take cover, you hide and stay there."

She nodded, and he prayed she meant it. He sent a text to John, too. Whatever happened, backup was on its way.

Nate slid through the opening in the chain-link fence and held it open for Mel to follow. There was no vision when he touched it this time. Maybe he was overreacting. He scanned the rotten rooftop, his weapon aimed and ready. Nothing.

He tipped his head toward the building and headed for the shadows. Mel followed close behind. At the inner door to the theater, he stopped. Glancing at her, he lowered the gun and reached for the handle with one hand.

Light exploded in his head. A man in a robe. His hood was up, faceless. He carried a metal canister with a pump on the top, like a sprayer for weed killer, and ran down the aisle to the wings of the stage. Right side.

And then the vision was gone.

"He's got a sprayer of some kind. Could be acid or God knows what. Wait for me here, okay?"

That hell-no wrinkle formed between her eyebrows. "You can't go in there alone. Wait for John to get here."

"The second that robed psycho hears those sirens blaring, he'll run. This is our chance to catch the guy."

She pressed her lips together, and then sighed. "Fine. But I'm coming with you. Someone has to call 9-1-

1 if things go wrong."

He shook his head. "Mel, *you're* the one he wants. Stay here." He searched her eyes. "Please."

She groaned, rolling her eyes. "You had to say *please.*"

He almost smiled. Brushing a kiss to her cheek, he whispered, "I'll be back soon."

By some miracle, the door hinges didn't squeak. He kept his Glock raised and ready as he crept down the aisle toward the stage. One beam of light came through a hole in the roof, like a cosmic spotlight on center stage. He was banking on the hooded guy still being off in the right wing of the stage. With any luck, Nate could come in behind him.

That was the plan anyway.

Life-and-death situations slowed his pulse, bending time. His focus grew as the tension mounted. He made his way up the steps on the side, his attention on the dusty curtains on the wings.

A faint thump froze him where he stood. Nate scanned for any sign of movement. Nothing. He steadied himself and continued. Once he ducked behind the first velvet curtain, the light vanished, plunging him into darkness. He held his breath, sliding his foot forward.

Click. He spun toward the sound. Three steps and there was a small flicker of light. A flame? "Put it down. Hands up," he said.

The robed man turned around, the light reflecting

off the gold mask. "Where is she?"

"None of your damned business. Now put your hands up where I can see them and walk slowly toward me."

The lighter clattered to the floor, taking the light with it. Nate ran blindly after the footsteps. By the time he got out of the wings, he jumped down the staircase and chased after the hooded man, praying Mel was hiding. He pumped his legs faster, widening his stride, but he'd never get to the doors to the lobby before the man in the Kronos mask.

His perp stretched his arms and hit the doors, but they didn't open. He fell backward. Before Nate could make a grab for him, he scrambled up, clamoring through the back row of broken, dusty seats. Nate pursued the worm in the hood, but his frame was bigger than the perp's and it slowed him down.

Sirens screamed in the distance. If they got here in time, he could flush the guy into the parking lot and he'd be trapped.

The gold mask turned his way before the guy pushed through the door. Nate plowed through the last few seats and opened the door. No perp and no Mel. His heart hammered. Had the masked bastard grabbed her?

"Mel?"

"I'm okay. He went that way. Outside."

Nate didn't hesitate. When he burst into the sunlight, the hooded man was already slipping through the cut in the fence. Nate sprinted for the opening, but the Kronos worshipper had a monumental lead. By the time Nate was through the fence, the stranger was out of the parking lot on foot. No car this time.

When Nate got to the street, the guy in the robe was gone. Nate scanned both directions. Nothing.

He bent over. "Fuck." He straightened and looked both ways again. "Dammit."

Two black-and-whites screeched into the lot. John jumped out of the first stopped car and hustled over. "What the hell happened?"

"Mel got an e-mail to meet her friend here, and I had a bad feeling. I was right."

John looked past him. "Is she here?"

Nate nodded. "Inside."

John walked away while Nate gave one of the officers a description, but if the guy took off the mask, it wouldn't help. He still hadn't seen the guy's face.

Mel was just getting up from the dirty floor when Nate's partner came in. "You all right?"

She nodded, dusting herself off. "Yeah. Is Nate okay?"

"Just pissed the guy got away." He looked past her and frowned. "What is that?"

She glanced over her shoulder at the back of the chair wedged under the door handles and the dusty table pressed against it. "I heard Nate tell the guy to put his hands up and then a scuffle, so I tried to slow him down a little."

Nate's partner smiled. Apparently he knew how, after all. Who knew?

"Nice work."

"Not really." She shrugged. "He still got away, right?"

"Yeah, but he didn't get *you*, which is really all my partner cared about."

Mel raised a brow. "Is this the part where you tell me to leave him alone?"

John turned to check the empty doorway, and then focused on her again. "I was an asshole, but I don't want to see him get into trouble. He's a great cop. Best partner I've ever had."

"For what it's worth, I think he's pretty amazing, too, and even if he pissed me off, I'd never try to get him fired. The world is a safer place with Nate Malone in it."

John almost smiled again. "I like the way you think."

Speak of the devil…

Nate came through the door, rushing past John, and embraced her. Tight. Suddenly he stiffened and stepped back, clearing his throat. "I'm glad you're safe." His gaze cut to his partner. "He had a lighter and a sprayer on the stage, but he didn't take them when he ran."

John nodded. "Let's check it out."

They moved her furniture barricade out of the way, and she followed them down the aisle toward the stage. John slowed his pace enough to fall in step with her behind Nate. "So how is it that anytime you're in danger, my partner is right there ready to swoop in?"

She stared at the back of Nate's head. "Cop's intuition, I guess."

"How'd you know, Malone?" John asked, trying a new tact.

Nate jogged up the stairs to the stage and turned back. "Her friend wouldn't say it was urgent without telling her what was wrong. It's not in Callie's nature. Subtle isn't her thing. I knew something was up."

Mel paused at the bottom of the stairs, a smile warming her lips. Nate had only met Callie a couple of times, but he had her personality nailed. He really was a great cop. Smart, strong, instinctive, and…hers. For now.

She rolled her eyes at herself and followed them up the stairs.

Nate and John had their flashlight apps glowing in the wings, inspecting the sprayer. A Bic lighter lay forgotten a few feet from the canister. John tugged a pair of latex gloves from his pocket.

"He was wearing black gloves," Nate said. "We won't get any prints." He knelt down, sniffing around the top of the sprayer. "Smells like gas."

Mel stared at the discarded lighter, heart pounding.

"He was going to set me on fire."

Nate got up and came to her side. "We're going to get him."

She looked up at him and frowned. "Hopefully before he gets me."

Until this moment, the danger had loomed in the distance. It was out there, but it hadn't seemed real. Seeing the gas sprayer and the lighter, knowing the wacko had hacked Callie's e-mail... Now the danger was real and right up on her ass. She pulled in a slow cleansing breath. If Nate hadn't insisted on coming with her, she would've been in an inferno right now.

Nate cupped her cheek. "Let's get out of here."

"Don't you need to get—"

"John, you got this?"

His partner nodded. "Yeah, we're good here."

"I'm going to call the techs and see if they can trace the IP address where the e-mail originated. Maybe we can track him that way."

"Sounds good. I'll let you know if we find anything here."

"Thanks, man." Nate caught her hand. "Let's go."

Once they were back in Nate's car, he turned toward her. "I know you're not going to like this, but you shouldn't go to work or any of the places this nutjob knows he can find you."

Deep inside, her muse wallowed in the fear and threat of danger. They'd never be able to find this guy. They didn't even know if it was only one guy. There could be many of them with that mask. She wasn't safe anywhere.

Nate's gut clenched with dread as Mel blinked and met his eyes. "No. What if that's what they want? If I stay put in one place, I'm an easier target, right?" She shook her head. "My students have their slam poetry coming up, and we've got to get the barbeque together for Maggie. I promised her."

"I can tell Maggie I have a big case. The party in the park can wait. She'll understand."

Mel took his hand. "She'll understand that she only matters when it's convenient. You told me yourself that she has no one. This is important." She broke eye contact. "They aren't going to kill me with hundreds of people watching."

He caught her chin, waiting for her eyes to meet his. "I won't let them hurt you."

She nodded slowly. "But I don't want them to hurt you, either."

"We're going to get to the bottom of this." He kissed her forehead. "Until then, I'm getting you some pepper spray and maybe a permit to carry concealed."

Mel chuckled, shaking her head. "I'll take the pepper spray, but I don't think I should have a gun. I don't even have a license. I'm more likely to shoot you or myself accidentally than a bad guy on purpose."

He rolled his eyes and started the car. "I'll teach you everything before I let you stick a pistol in your purse."

She didn't look convinced. "We'll see."

Mel called Callie on the way over to let her know about the e-mail, and by the time they drove up to her place, all the muses were gathered in the living room. Nate's stomach churned, but he smiled as one of them hopped up from the table. Her long, dark hair was pulled back in a ponytail, and her hazel eyes sparkled behind her black-rimmed glasses.

"You must be Mel's Guardian. I'm Clio, the Muse of History." She grinned, a little pink lighting up her cheeks. "I'm the one who found out you existed."

He shook her hand. Firm, all business. "Nice to meet you, Clio. I'm Nate."

Clio spun around to the table. "Everyone, this is Nate, Mel's *Guardian*. They're real!"

He caught Mel's eye, silently pleading for an escape route. She smiled, but made no move to drag him out. The next few minutes were a blur of names and muses. As a detective, he used memory tricks for attaching names to faces and places. While they chatted about e-mail passwords and security cameras, he glanced around the table making such connections.

Callie, the Muse of Epic Poetry, he'd already met more than once, so she was easy. Next up, Clio, the Muse of History, and judging by the three books under her elbow, she loved to read. Beside her was Trinity, the Muse of Music. He recognized her black hair with an angled cut and her dark eyes. This was the woman who played guitar when Mel's class sang the blues.

The woman beside her introduced herself as Trin's roommate, the Muse of Lyrics. He struggled for the name—Erica. She was the only woman at the table with fiery red hair, brighter than Mel's deep auburn. Filing that away, the next trio was made up of Polly, the money behind their theater project and the Muse of Hymns; Tera, the Muse of Dance; and Thalia, the Muse of Comedy. She'd be easy to remember, her laughter was so unique and clear; you couldn't help but smile.

Finally his gaze rested on Mel, the Muse of Tragic Poetry. His. All the women at the table were beautiful, and probably talented in their own way, but Mel was the only one he ached to touch. Her smiles were gifts, and her passion for life and love for her work and kids, it all came together into a woman who inspired him to be a better man, to take risks. She lured him closer to the dangerous cliff of emotion and enticed him to jump.

He walked farther into the room and stood behind Mel's chair. He rubbed her shoulders, watching Callie.

"If these guys in Kronos masks want to stop us, we have to assume they want to kill inspiration, to stop inspiring mankind." Callie shook her head. "We can't let that happen."

She went on to talk security cameras on her house, as well as the theater. Polly was happy to support both projects. Then she brought up the permits for the roof. Suddenly she looked up at him. "Do you have an update on the attempted bombing of our theater?"

He straightened. "Our lead at the docks was murdered, but so far, our investigation keeps pointing to Belkin Oil. Any idea why an oil company might not want your theater to open?"

Callie shrugged and looked around the table. "Anyone have any ideas?"

Trinity shifted in her chair, even just speaking, her voice was clear like a crystal bell. "I don't know anyone at Belkin Oil, but I dated a guy in college named Belkin."

Callie raised a brow. "But he's not at Belkin Oil?"

She shook her head. "Not that I know of. We lost touch, but he didn't live around here. His family was from down south someplace."

"So that's a dead end." Callie glanced around. "Anyone else?"

Mel tapped her fingernail on the table. "I keep coming back to what Nate said about Kronos and the Titans. I know it sounds insane, but what if they really are trying to free the Titans from the center of the Earth?"

Clio patted her hand. "That's a myth, Mel. The Earth's core is made of magma. It's not a prison for Titans."

Mel shook her head. "Myths usually grow from a real human problem that couldn't be explained. What if the magma *is* the prison?"

Callie tilted her head slightly. "So if the Titans really were trapped in magma at the Earth's core and someone wanted to get them out…"

"They'd need to drill," Mel finished, reaching up to touch his hand on her shoulder. "If Nate's right and there is a Kronos cult, the only people in town capable of releasing him would be at Belkin Oil."

CHAPTER 16

THE TORCHES BLAZED as their leader raised his hands to the sky. "Our father, Uranus, we call on your help. Guide our hand in our mission."

Their leader nodded, and they all lowered their torches to the larger pyre of wood, sending the smoke up to the heavens. Ted stood on his father, their leader's right side. On his left was Ben.

He had clawed his way through their ranks onto the platform, elevating himself above the others. Ted could imagine his smug smile behind the golden face of Kronos. Bastard.

Once the fire blazed to life, his father lifted his hands again. "The communication is open. Speak freely."

"The Muse of Tragic Poetry still lives," Ted blurted out. "Perhaps it's time we find a new enforcer."

Murmurs blossomed through the group. Ben stepped forward. "The muse is protected by a police detective, but I discovered a weakness for them both."

Their leader's deep baritone cut through the popping of the blazing wood. "And that is?"

"A little girl. Her name is Maggie."

Their leader turned to face the Order. "Tend the fire while I have a private moment with our enforcer."

He growled to Ted. "Come with us."

Behind his mask, Ted grinned. He would love seeing Ben out on his ass. He hadn't told his father that he'd already been grooming Ben's replacement. Bryce could follow orders without a football stadium–sized ego.

Behind the platform, they walked a few paces into the trees, and removed their golden masks. Ted Belkin, Sr. narrowed his eyes at Ben. "What are you planning?"

Ben cleared his throat. "I will grab the girl after school and arrange a trade—Melanie Jacoby for Maggie."

Belkin, Sr. pursed his lips and crossed his arms. "Then the detective and the girl will know about the Order."

"I'll tie up the loose ends, sir," Ben said.

"Oh, please." Ted groaned. "The police are *still* sniffing around about the C-4 in the theater. We can't keep having loose ends."

Belkin, Sr. held up a hand to silence him. Ted shut up, glaring at Ben.

His father turned to Ben. "We have a mission to free the Titans, to bring about the Golden Age of Man once more. We are the *heroes* in this story. Heroes don't kidnap children. They also don't cut a workingman's throat while his wife is sleeping in the next room. This has to stop. We're not murderers. The muses have the potential of blocking our cause. They are our *only* enemy. Do we understand each other?"

"Yes." Ben tipped his chin up a notch. "But there are casualties in any revolution, sir."

"No!" Belkin, Sr. grabbed a handful of Ben's robe and yanked him close. His voice became a guttural growl. "Find another way."

He shoved Ben back. "I won't cover for any more 'casualties.' The muse dies; no one else. Am I clear?"

Ben nodded slowly. "Crystal."

"Good." Belkin, Sr. pointed at Ted. "Keep an eye on him. Be a leader, not a stool pigeon." His father put on his mask and walked back to the platform.

Ted narrowed his eyes at Ben. "One more mistake and you're finished."

NATE STOOD ON the edge of the lake beside the crane. The silver Honda Accord groaned as it rose from the water. A guy on a fishing boat had seen the sun glint off the silver roof and called the police. Nate crossed his arms, willing the crane to go faster. Part of him was hoping there'd be a body inside. Maybe the guy in the gold mask lost control of his car and drowned with it.

Mel would be safe.

Then what? She'd move back to Callie's place, and he'd get back to his regular life.

His empty life.

He clenched his teeth as the water drained from the Accord's doors and windows. Until he met Mel, he hadn't realized he'd been missing anything.

She turned everything upside down.

And dammit, she was the best part of every day. He looked forward to seeing her at the end of the day, touching her, hearing her laugh. Shit, he'd even looked at puppies online.

Mel and her sisters were busy planning the barbeque at the park for Sunday afternoon. Maggie had given away all her invitations. John was coming, too, to help Nate keep an eye out for any sign of gold masks.

The car sat on all four wheels on the ground, but it was already clear and empty. Nate opened the driver's side door. Water sloshed out, and he slapped his hand on the roof.

"Dammit. Just one fucking lead would be nice."

Once the car finished leaking, he leaned inside. A piece of wood kept the accelerator down so the vehicle "drowning" hadn't been accidental. He went around to the other side and opened the glove compartment. More water, and a few papers stuck together.

A registration card. Better than nothing. And waterlogged receipts. He carefully separated them, but one caught his eye. The credit card name read Belkin Oil.

He jogged back to his car, calling to the tow truck driver. "Take it to impound."

Back at the station, he dried out the papers from

the glove box, and John leaned over his shoulder. "The DMV says the car was sold for cash. New owner didn't change the title yet."

"Another dead end." Nate held up the gas receipt. "But this is an arrow pointing to our friends at Belkin Oil. Again."

John took the receipt. "Maybe someone at Belkin bought that car."

"We could take some of the employee pictures over to the woman who sold the car. She might be able to pick out Lewis Gold."

John slapped his back. "I'll get them together, and we can set up a meeting."

"I'll track the previous owner down and get her to come in." Nate's pulse pounded in his ears. Finally, a solid lead.

He grabbed his cell and texted Mel.

Might have a lead. Can I pick you up after work?

After he hit "Send," he stared at the phone. If this panned out and they made an arrest, he didn't want Mel to move out. He wanted to see her every day. But what if she didn't want that?

These were questions he'd never faced before. This was exactly why relationships were off-limits. He got up from his desk and headed for the door, desperate for fresh air. His chest constricted as he paced the sidewalk. He should just solve this, know she's safe, and let her get on with her life.

His heart clenched. What about his life? He'd laughed more in the past few weeks than he had in years. And while he'd never had a shortness of women in his bedroom, no one ever turned him on like Mel did. She didn't need makeup, or sexy underwear, or perfume. Just her voice, her smile, and the way she looked at him.

He had nothing to hide when he was with her. And somehow it didn't make him feel weak.

His phone buzzed.

Only if you promise to feed me. I'm starving today!

Two sentences and his panic lightened. Nate chuckled and sent a text back.

Donato's on me. See you soon.

MEL STARED AT the text. Donato's was a fancy Italian place. She looked down at her black jeans and emerald-green blouse with black buttons. Hmm. The lead Nate found must be huge.

Her heart dropped. What if he makes an arrest? Will he expect her to move out? Donato's was probably to celebrate getting his place back again.

Suddenly she didn't care that she was underdressed. Realistically, she should be thrilled to be out of danger. But the danger was what had brought Nate into her life.

She wasn't ready to give him up yet.

And what about the barbeque this weekend? She'd go through with it for Maggie regardless, but it was going to be painful if Nate was there and she couldn't touch him.

The bell rang and students filed into her room. Brian came up and set a copy of his poem on her desk. She glanced at it and up to his face. "You didn't have to bring a copy for me."

He nodded. "Yeah, I did. My mom told me to be sure you looked at it first so I don't get in trouble for reading it today."

"Why would you be in trouble?" She scanned the paper and found the colorful language near the end. "Oh."

"So can I read it?"

Brian's dad had left him and his mom a couple of years prior, and he'd responded by clamming up. Being the tough guy. Getting him to write a poem was a miracle, having him ready to share it, and slam it with the class was a gift that wouldn't come around again if she shut him down now.

Besides, she was in a cursing kind of mood.

She lifted her gaze. "Lose the F-Bomb and you can keep the others, but warn everyone first so they have the option to leave if they find it offensive."

He caught himself before he let a smile slip through. "Thanks, Ms. Jacoby."

She called roll and stepped to the front. The desks were moved back a few feet, giving the poets space to work the room. They'd watched some slam poets on YouTube this week to prepare, and today would be volunteers only. No mandatory readings, but she was pleased to see more than half the class had signed up, including Brian.

"Remember our rules. Respect for the poet at all times. You can clap, cheer, cry—all emotions are welcome. Be open and support your classmates. Slamming isn't easy. Got it?"

Lots of nods and the first student got up. Some nervous giggles, but overall, she nailed it. As more went up and shared their scars, their passions, and their heartbreaks, her eyes welled with tears of pride.

Finally, Brian took center stage. "Yo, I got some language in here so you got a problem, you better step out."

He waited. None of them left.

Brian found his rhythm, and the room fell silent. He shouted and cursed, but it was the soft lines when his voice trembled that ripped her heart out. The quiet moments when he admitted his pain and wished he could see his dad one last time, aching for closure he would probably never get.

When he finished, all the air sucked from the room. He froze. And one set of hands clapped, followed by another, until all the students in the room were on their feet cheering.

And Brian smiled.

Mel wiped a tear from her cheek, cheering right along with the rest of the class. Kids hugged and high-fived him as he made his way back to his spot.

A poem on its own might not change a life, but a moment like this could.

The bell rang, and she turned to find Nate at her door. Her heart stuttered. He moved out of the doorway so the steady stream of students could rush out, but his gaze never left her face, not for a second. How long had he been there?

Once the room was empty, he crossed to her desk. "You're amazing."

She shook her head, heat flushing her cheeks, and she stacked the papers on her desk. "I didn't expect you to be so prompt."

She wasn't ready for this talk yet. If it was going to be the one she expected—the one where he told her it's safe to go back to Callie's—she didn't want to hear it. His finger caught her chin, drawing her attention up to him.

"Why wouldn't I be?"

She shrugged, wishing she didn't love staring up into his eyes. "I don't know. You have a lead so I thought you'd be chasing it, lose track of time, call to cancel—"

He stopped her rambling with a tender kiss. When he pulled back, a smile tugged at his lips. "What's wrong? Your glass half-empty is running away with you."

She took a step back. "It's silly." She grabbed her bag and hooked it on her shoulder. "Let's get going before we have to get a dinner reservation."

His expression sobered. "Mel, talk to me."

She leaned against the edge of her desk and crossed her arms. "I'm freaked out because you wanted to take me someplace fancy."

He puzzled over that for a second and finally chuckled. "I thought you'd be excited. I wanted to celebrate, that's all."

"But what are we celebrating?"

Now he looked as uncomfortable as some of her students when she made them read aloud. Shit. She was right. She balled her hands into fists behind her back, trying to hold herself together.

Nate blew out a slow breath and lifted his gaze to her face. "I wanted to celebrate the lead, and then I hoped I'd be celebrating that when this is over, you would stay. With me."

Surprise didn't begin to describe her sudden relief. She rushed toward him, and he took her in his arms, holding her as if he'd never let her go.

He kissed her hair and whispered, "Is that a yes?"

She nodded and pulled back to see his face. "Yes. I thought you were going to tell me I'd have to move soon."

"I was worried you'd be relieved to get back to Callie's place."

She shook her head slowly. "In spite of the fear for my life, I've never been happier."

Something in his eyes, in the way he looked at her like she was all that mattered, made her knees weak. "Me neither."

"Now that that's settled, how about we celebrate with Italian?" She grinned.

He chuckled and kissed her again. "You read my mind."

NATE LIFTED HIS champagne glass, clinking it against Mel's. "Here's to hoping this lead pans out."

The restaurant was dimly lit with a candle on every table. And although it was just after three in the afternoon, the candlelight sparkled in her dark eyes. She made him smile, and he loved hearing her laugh. Even the silence was comfortable.

Knowing she wanted to stay after the case was over had lifted a weight off his shoulders. It also opened a door inside his heart. A door he'd been terrified to open his entire adult life.

After their meal at Donato's, he walked her out to the car. The shadows lengthened, the sun dipping low on the horizon. "Can I ask you something?"

Mel nodded. "Sure."

"This theater you're all trying to restore… Why would it be such a threat to followers of Kronos?"

She stopped walking. He turned to look down into her eyes. Her smile stole his breath.

"You saw Brian in my class today. That kind of inspiration can change the world, Nate. Our theater isn't just going to show *Oklahoma*. It's going to be a meeting place for inspiration. We'll have poets, musicians, dancers, and communities that are trying to make the world better; they'll all come together in our theater. We'll hang art to inspire, too. The human race will find new clean energy, cures for cancer, and hope. It's all about inspiration."

He cupped her cheek, memorizing every curve of her face. "You're…I…" He kissed her before words fell from his mouth that he wasn't ready to share yet. Her soft lips caressed his as his pulse raced. He almost… It bubbled up unconsciously.

Love.

And something else, something she'd said. His subconscious lingered on her words: *Clean energy.*

He broke the kiss. "Energy. That's it! Your theater would be a threat to an oil company. They don't want clean energy."

"And they'd have the drilling equipment to…"

"Free the Titans." He took her hand and hustled to the car. "We're hoping the woman who sold the silver Honda Accord can identify an employee from Belkin Oil as the man who bought it from her. It won't be enough to charge anyone yet, but we'll have a man to watch and when he makes a mistake, we'll be there to catch him."

Mel buckled her seat belt. "Just don't get so wrapped up that you miss Maggie's barbeque this weekend."

He shook his head with a smile. "No chance."

Mel told him all the party details on the way home. It wasn't miniature golf, but hopefully she'd like it. As he passed his street, Mel watched the sign pass by.

"You missed the turn."

"We're not going home yet." He glanced her way.

"We're not?"

He shook his head. When he got to the light, he turned her way. "Hope you like to dance."

Mel grinned. "Love it. I didn't know you were a dancer."

"I can hold my own."

She chuckled. "I would've dressed hotter today if I knew I'd be going to Donato's and dancing after work."

"I would've warned you, but I'm winging it tonight."

She raised a brow. "Improvising looks good on you, Malone."

He tipped his head back, laughing. She made loving her way too easy. Just thinking the word made his palms sweat.

In the parking lot, he took her hand, his fingers twining with hers. Everything about her fit him—her tall frame, her dark eyes, her voice, and her body.

But it was her heart that mesmerized him. They

stepped into the shadowed light of the club, the bass roaring out of the speakers and pounding a steady beat. She grinned. "I love this song!"

He followed her onto the dance floor. It was early enough that there weren't writhing bodies bumping them. Mel moved with the music, fluid and sensual, and already his blood was pumping below his belt. She came closer, her thigh between his so they could rock together, grinding slowly. She slid her arms around his waist, pulling him close to her.

Her lips brushed his ear. "Every girl on this dance floor wants you."

He glanced around and back to her eyes. "Tough. I only want you."

"Lucky me." She looked up at him from under her lashes, and it was all he could do not to carry her to a dark corner and kiss her until she forgot her name.

He bent to rest his forehead against hers. "This was a mistake." Her smile faltered, and he shook his head. "Too many people. We need someplace more private."

Her grin returned. "Maybe your place?"

He nodded and scooped her up into his arms, enjoying the squeak of surprise as he carried her off the dance floor.

CHAPTER 17

Back at Nate's place, Mel started up her iPod in his bedroom. She turned to find Nate unbuttoning his shirt. Heat smoldered low in her belly. "We're getting comfortable?"

The hunger and desire in his gaze was all the answer she needed. He let his shirt fall to the ground, and her heart thumped. He didn't even hesitate to expose his scars. She smiled. He trusted her whether he realized it or not.

As soon as her top hit the floor, he wrapped her in his arms. His hot skin against her bare chest sent a shiver through her body. As the song ended, his hands slid up her back to unfasten her bra. She stepped back long enough to slip it free, and then he tugged her close to him again.

His lips brushed her shoulder. "Much better."

She nodded, closing her eyes as they swayed together. The song faded out, and the next one kicked in with a vengeance. Nate froze for a second and raised his head to meet her eyes.

She laughed. She couldn't help it. Bonnie Tyler's "Holding Out for a Hero" blasted through the room.

"This is a little up-tempo." She started to pull away to change it. "It's on shuffle. I can find something slower."

"Don't." Nate held her tighter. "I want to be that for you. Your Guardian, your hero."

"You are." She bit her lower lip to keep the three words in her heart from escaping. Sliding one hand from around his neck, she traced his jawline. "You make me very happy."

"Good." He grinned, grinding slowly with her.

His erection pressed against her, making her heart pound in answer. She loved knowing he wanted her. The song ended and he took her hand, walking toward the bed, when Etta James stopped them both in their tracks.

At last my love has come along.

Mel didn't know where to look, but Nate bent to kiss her lips and took her hand. Next thing she knew, they were dancing slowly, their tongues twining together as the lyrics wrapped them in a magical embrace.

He broke the kiss, resting his forehead against hers, his eyes staring directly into her soul. As Etta belted out the last line, Nate's gritty whisper stopped time.

"I don't know how this happened…" He paused, searching her eyes. "I love you, Mel."

Her knees turned to rubber, but he held her so tight she knew she'd never fall. She swallowed the lump of emotion choking her and whispered, "I love you, too."

He chuckled and somehow managed to look happy, relieved, and terrified all at once. That honesty melted her heart. He had finally let her in, and she'd do all she could to protect that trust. To love him.

They collapsed on the bed and made quick work of their pants. He grabbed a condom from the drawer and hovered over her. Mel shook her head. "Not so fast." She rolled him over and smiled down at him. "I get to be on top this time."

He stared up at her, sliding his hands up from her waist to cup her breasts. "God, you're beautiful."

She closed her eyes, drinking in the way he teased her nipples. Leaning forward over him, she kissed his lips. "You make me feel beautiful."

Slowly, she lowered herself, moaning as he slid inside her. Nate ran his hands down her body, gripping her thighs. He lifted his head, kissing her, hungry, greedy.

Breathless, he growled, "I want this to last all night, but I also want to flip you over and pound into you until we can't speak."

She smiled, lifting her hips, drawing him nearly out before slowly coming down again. His grip tightened, and he thrust up hard in answer. She trembled and worked into him faster. Gods, he was made for her.

Suddenly, Nate's large hands moved up her back, holding her tightly, and he rolled them over. She laughed into his kiss.

He pulled back, smiling. "Sorry. I couldn't take any

more teasing."

He slid his hand between them until his fingertips found the perfect spot. He rubbed in time with his thrusts, coaxing her closer to her peak. She gripped him tighter, her nails digging into his back as her body tightened. Nate growled, pushing up into her, his hips slamming against hers. Just as he shuddered, her inner muscles clenched around him.

For a moment, they were both still. Finally, she sucked in a breath. "I can't move."

He chuckled, shivering above her. "Good."

Mel grinned. "That was *way better* than good."

"Coming from an English teacher."

Mel laughed. "Cut her a break, the English teacher just came."

Nate kissed her and slowly slid himself free. "Be right back."

She enjoyed the view of his naked backside and crawled up to the top of the bed. He returned and got into bed beside her, and she rolled onto her side, resting on his chest. "How are you doing?"

He smiled. "I'm in love with an incredible woman." He shook his head, sobering a little. "I'm hanging in there."

Honesty again. Such a gift.

She kissed his chest. "Thanks for letting me into your heart."

He tucked her hair behind her ear. "You walked in like you had a key."

"The gods were kind to me when they made me your muse."

BEING WITHOUT HIS robe and gold mask made it difficult to focus. Whenever Ben donned the hooded visage of the Order, he lost his human identity. He became *the enforcer*, bringing them closer to the Golden Age of Man. He could face the tasks required without being burdened by the laws of man and the morals of humanity.

So hanging around a busy park in the middle of the afternoon was tough for him. Though, while distancing himself from his duty would be a challenge, this would work.

Their leader had handicapped him by forbidding him from kidnapping the little girl, but he'd come up with a work-around. It had taken a few days, but now he had Melanie Jacoby's cell phone number. Soon she would come to him willingly, alone. And he would do what must be done.

NATE PULLED UP to the park to find Mel and her sisters already had a Darth Vader piñata hanging from a tree branch and two tables decorated with tablecloths and balloons.

Maggie's eyes widened as she removed her seat belt. "Wow! It's not even my birthday." She looked over at him, beaming. "You must've taken Mel to minature golf!"

He chuckled. "Didn't have to, she likes you so much."

"Another mom and dad came to see me," Maggie told him, her smile faltering a little. "But I guess they didn't like me as much as Mel does."

His heart clenched. Mrs. Gaines had told him about the meeting. The potential family thought Maggie was too old for their daughter. They hadn't "meshed." But how did you explain that to a seven-year-old?

And how could anyone not "mesh" with Maggie? He couldn't fathom it. "They didn't deserve you, Maggie."

"Why can't I stay with you, Uncle Nate?"

Mel was coming toward the car. He willed her to move faster.

"We've talked about this." He sighed. "I work too much, and besides, you need a mom, too."

Mel opened the door, and they both stared at her.

She started to frown. "Did I interrupt an important meeting?"

Maggie looked back at Nate. She didn't say anything. Yet.

Before he could get a word in, Maggie turned back to Mel and grinned. "We were just talking about how I could live with Uncle Nate, but he works too much, so I'd need a mom."

On that note, she scrambled free of the car and ran to the tables.

Mel watched her go and chuckled. "She's an evil supergenius."

Nate sighed. "I'd adopt her myself if I could." He shook his head. "She had another meeting with a couple yesterday. They passed."

Mel frowned. "How could anyone pass up Maggie?"

"That's what I always think." He got out and came around to her side. "Anyway, she's a little fixated on finding new parents at the moment."

Mel nodded, but she didn't say anything. Finally, she pointed to the barbeque. "We need you to fire up the grill. I have burgers and hot dogs over there."

He scanned the park. Sunday afternoon was busy with two rented jumpy castles, plenty of families, and people walking their dogs. No signs of gold masks. He rubbed his shoulder. No pain.

Maybe they'd actually get to enjoy the day.

This week, his latest lead turned into another dead end. They'd shown the woman who sold the silver Honda the pictures of every employee of Belkin Oil. She didn't recognize any of them. They were able to make a composite from her description, which was good, but so far, no hits.

His gut still told him Belkin was behind the C-4,

and possibly involved in Nia's death, and Mel's brushes with the man in the Kronos mask. But without any hard evidence, he still couldn't make any arrests. They must've hired out a hit man.

Either way, a day with Maggie and Mel in the park was a welcome respite from the frustration of the case. He checked his phone. John and the rest of the guests would be there in a half hour. Maggie was laughing with Mel while they filled more helium balloons. Trinity strummed her guitar, tuning it for a sing-along, and the others worked on setting up face painting and a spot where the kids could color.

With any luck, Maggie would make lots of new friends today.

Maggie laughed with her whole body, and Mel couldn't get enough. It was impossible not to smile at her. When the kids started arriving, she greeted each one with a hug followed by pointing out all the activities they had planned.

Callie helped Polly with face painting, and Clio was manning the coloring station.

Mel kept watching Nate at the grill, turning hot dogs and talking to John. Yes, the danger was still out there somewhere, but for today, the sun was up, the kids were having fun, and she was in love.

She tried to focus on that and just enjoy it, but the

damned muse inside of her wouldn't leave her alone. Nothing could be this perfect. She scanned the area while she folded the bandana to blindfold the piñata smackers. Nothing seemed wrong, though. There were two other parties with inflatable jumpers, kids everywhere, moms with strollers, a few dog walkers, but no gold masks, no black robes.

Nate caught her eye and called over to her. "Everything okay?"

She nodded in answer but wished she felt more certain.

Maggie ran up, eyes wide, as Mel laid the blindfold on the table next to the bat. "Mel! Lexi and me are racing to the swings. Can you judge?"

"Sure." She walked toward the finish line, the sun warming her back. The girls got ready and then sprinted toward her. They were neck and neck until Lexi took a tumble.

Maggie stopped and looked at the swings, then back at her fallen friend. Mel held her breath. Maggie turned and jogged over to Lexi, offering her a hand. She helped her sweep the grass off her clothes, and they giggled as they walked together the rest of the way.

Mel smiled, releasing her pent-up breath. Maggie was making friends.

After face painting and games, lunch was almost ready.

"Can we swing a little more?" Maggie asked.

Nate gave her the ten-minute signal from the grill.

She turned back to Maggie. "Sure. We'll call you when the food is ready."

As the girls neared the swings, Mel's cell phone chimed. She had a text from an unknown number. She opened it and her hands started to tremble as she scrolled through pictures of Maggie in the park followed by a single text.

> *She's in the center of my rifle sight right now. Come to the library next door. Alone. Now. If the detective is with you…Maggie dies.*

CHAPTER 18

MEL SQUINTED INTO the sun. Even with her hand shading her brow, she couldn't see the library roof clearly enough. The photos came from that direction, though. Her heart hammered in her chest.

There must be something I can do. Think.

Her fingers shook on the screen as she typed.

I need a minute. If I don't tell him I'm going, he'll follow me.

She took two steps back toward the party area, and her cell rang.

"Keep this line open," a cold, masculine voice commanded. "Hang up and I shoot."

"I'm coming. Please leave her alone." Her pulse fluttered as she passed the swings where Maggie and her new friend were playing.

"Mel, where are you going?" Maggie shouted.

"Just have to get a book at the library. I'll be right back." She didn't look at them but kept her eyes on the building ahead. Like a lamb to the slaughter.

"That's it," he purred in her ear. "Keep walking and she'll be just fine. You're the one we want. They don't need to be involved."

Mel's pulse raced, sweat coating her palms. She needed a plan. But there was no time. Every stride brought her closer to the person on the other end of the line—the man who killed Nia. Now she would be next unless she could come up with something fast.

So it was her or Maggie.

And Maggie wasn't an option.

At least this way, Nate and Maggie would be safe and off the crazed Kronos fanatics' radar. Her heart ached. She'd never in her life wanted to live more than she did right now. The damned irony wasn't lost on her.

"Mel?" Nate jogged up next to her. "Is everything okay? Where are you going?"

Oh shit. She kept her eyes on the library, praying the shooter would wait. She lowered the cell phone without disconnecting the call. "Just going to see what the library has handy that I can read to the party-goers after the piñata."

"A book?" He frowned, trying to get into her line of vision. "You planned this whole day already. Story time wasn't on the list."

"Plans change. I'll be right back."

Nate followed her gaze to the library, assessing, then back to her. "Talk to me. What's going on?"

She couldn't look at him. He wasn't going to let this be easy. She wanted to tell him a rifle was aimed at Maggie right now, to show him the photos on her phone, but anything she said would be heard by the gunman, and if she ended the call, Maggie would pay.

Her stomach twisted as the realization dawned. She needed him to leave and let her walk away alone. To save Maggie, she would have to hurt Nate.

Mel forced her eyes from the library roof, praying Nate would figure out what was really happening. They hadn't been together long enough for little silent signals to develop. He'd only just let her into his heart, told her he loved her.

In the distance, Maggie giggled. Pure joy. Mel needed to protect her. And if she lived, she'd make it up to Nate.

Be strong.

She set her jaw and forced the words out. "I need a break, okay?" She rested her hand on her hip, heart pounding in her ears. "Why don't you hang out with Maggie? I'll meet up with you later."

He frowned. "What am I supposed to tell her when she asks for you?"

"I don't know. Tell her I got sick?" Her stomach tied in knots. "Take her home for all I care."

"Take her home?" Confusion lined his face. "This party was your idea."

Please, Nate. Get her out of the rifle's range.

"I'm well aware of that, but it turns out I wasn't as ready to pretend we're a happy family as I thought I was. I need some breathing room. I'll meet you at your place later."

His shoulders tightened, and she prayed he'd do as she asked. If Maggie was out of the equation, Mel could run.

He crossed his arms. "You didn't bring your car. How will you get there?"

"Enough with the inquisition, okay?" She raised her voice, desperate for him to go. "Maggie is *your* responsibility, not mine." She swallowed hard and braced herself. "It's easier to love someone when you're naked in his arms. I didn't sign up for an instant family."

He almost flinched. The surprise and hurt in his eyes made her physically ill.

"I don't understand." He shook his head. "I thought you…" His words died on his lips as a well-worn mask of indifference settled over him. "Never mind. I should've known better. Go. I'll take care of Maggie."

He stormed away, widening the distance between them as her heart tore in two. Tears stung her eyes. Seeing the way he'd closed himself off from her, and knowing it was her own fault, seared her, but not with sorrow.

With rage.

This had to stop. She wouldn't be played like a puppet.

She lifted the phone to her ear. "Why not just shoot me now?"

"No questions. Keep walking."

She glanced back at the party. Nate was back at the

grill. He didn't take Maggie out of the park. She didn't really expect him to, but it was her only hope. There was no other way out now. She'd have to give herself up. Two more steps, but when she looked back this time, Nate was rubbing his shoulder. His green eyes met hers.

His mark. He would know she was in danger.

She spun around before he came after her and walked to the corner of the library. "Okay, I'm here. Leave Maggie alone."

Her instinct to run and save herself overwhelmed her, flooding her with adrenaline and fear. But somewhere deep inside, a voice whispered that Nate would come. Even though she'd hurt him, he'd still come for her because he was her Guardian. Regardless of how betrayed and pissed he might be right now, he wouldn't let them kill her.

A man in a black suit and dark glasses approached her, grabbing her upper arm hard. "Give me your phone."

She handed it to him, and he raised it to his ear. "I've got her."

He ended the call and pocketed her cell. She'd get it back after Nate kicked his ass.

The muse inside her railed against the spark of hope, but Mel held her head high as the guy shoved her into the back of a black SUV. Nate might not ever trust her again, but he'd still save her life. She had to believe that or she'd lose her mind.

And for now, that was all she had left.

Nate glared at Mel as she continued toward the library. What the hell happened? She'd seemed so happy earlier. He reached for the tongs to turn the hot dogs and burned his fingers on the grill.

"Dammit!" The pain from the burn snapped him back in time, reminded him he was nothing. Damaged goods. Mel could do better.

Maybe she finally figured it out, too.

He lifted his gaze, and she turned around. For a moment, their eyes met and his birthmark throbbed. He frowned, reaching up to rub his shoulder. When he looked back, she was gone.

His wounded heart was glad. It was easier to forget someone if he couldn't see her. Forget her and never make this mistake again.

But his shoulder hurt like hell, burning more than his red, angry fingers.

John came over. "You're turning the dogs into charcoal, Malone."

"Take over for me." He handed his partner the tongs. "I'll be right back."

Nate walked toward the library, replaying his last conversation with Mel. It made no sense. She'd made him believe he was a Guardian, her hero. Why? Why do that and walk away?

He had too many questions and not enough answers.

And for the first time in his life, he believed he deserved them. He wasn't nothing, goddammit. He was a good detective and a good man. Mel helped him recognize that and see past his scars.

The closer he got to the library the less his heart ached and the more his gut burned. He would get her out of whatever mess she was in, and then he'd demand an explanation. By the time he neared the corner of the building, his shoulder was throbbing. She was definitely in danger.

He boxed up his emotions and ran.

At the back of the library, he stopped and checked in both directions. No sign of Mel. He grabbed the pole on the corner of the building and a vision bloomed. A man in black gripped her arm and held her cell phone. He walked her around to the front and into a black SUV. Nate struggled to see its plate number.

But then the vision faded.

"Shit."

He jogged around the front of the building, scanning the lot. Nothing. He was too late.

"No, no, no…"

At the curb, he leaned on a parking meter and Mel's face filled his head. The man in black shoved her into the SUV and raced around to the driver's seat. Another man in jeans and a black T-shirt hustled to the passenger door, a rifle at his side.

It vanished as quickly as it had come. "Dammit!"

His heart pounded in his ears. The visions weren't enough. If he couldn't figure out where they were taking her, they would kill her. And without a plate number to call in, he was fucked. He raked his hand through his hair, struggling to think straight.

Then it came to him. Thinking was the problem.

He ran back to his car, calling to John, "Watch Maggie for me. I'll be back."

John waved the tongs in reply, and Nate started his car. He pulled out and took a deep breath, anything to quiet his scattered thoughts and clear his head. One time he'd accidentally jogged to the theater and stopped the Kronos cult from blowing it up, and another time as he'd driven home, he'd ended up at Callie's place instead. He just needed to trust it would work this time, too.

Fighting the urge to try to deduce a potential destination, he focused on Maggie and how happy she'd been all day. He wanted her to have that every day. Mel had been right about the barbeque. Maggie was making new friends. There was still a chance he could save that little girl when he couldn't do the same for her mom.

Up ahead he caught a glimpse of a black SUV as it turned a corner. His pulse surged. It was working. He gripped the wheel tighter and punched the accelerator. After he made the turn, he eased up on the gas. If he got too close, they might spot his tail.

There was no guarantee this was even the right

SUV, but the burning in his shoulder told him it was, and after the past few crazy weeks, he trusted his new senses. He didn't have any other choice anyway.

The SUV parked at a warehouse with a For Lease sign on the wall. Nate pulled into a nearby alley and held his breath, watching in the rearview mirror. The man in black got out of the driver's side and opened the back door. He yanked Mel outside. She stumbled, and Nate tensed. If they hurt her, he wasn't sure he'd be able to stop at just arresting them.

The two men looked up and down the street and then hauled her inside.

Nate got out of his car, drew his Glock from his shoulder holster, and made his way across the street.

MEL'S HEART SANK the moment they pulled her out of the car. There was no sign of Nate. She'd been certain he'd come for her. Maybe he'd been too late. Or maybe he had done what she'd told him to and had taken Maggie home.

Either way, she wouldn't get a chance to explain that every word she'd said to him was utter bullshit; to tell him she'd never been happier than when she was spending the day as a family at the park with him, Maggie, and her sisters.

At least Maggie is safe, Mel reminded herself. That would have to be enough.

Inside, a man stood alone at the far end of the dimly lit warehouse. He wore a golden mask of Kronos and a black hood. She stopped, heart palpitating as her legs turned rubbery. The man in dark glasses shoved her forward.

Her eyes burned, but she willed back the tears. She wouldn't give these psychos the satisfaction. "Why are you doing this?" Her voice trembled. "I haven't done anything to you."

The man at the end shook his head. "On the contrary. Every day that you are alive, your inspiration slows our progress."

"Progress of what?" she shouted. "Killing innocent women like Nia?" Saying her friend's name, hearing it echo back, stoked the fire in her belly. "She was kind and full of light. The world was better with her in it."

"Enough talking." He raised one hand. "Bring her to me."

Something glinted in the thin beam of sunlight filtering in—a knife of some sort. Mel struggled, stomping on Dark Glasses's foot. He let go. She spun for the door, but he caught her hair, jerking her back so hard she saw stars. She landed on her ass. She looked around, trying to get her bearings back, and realized the guy with the rifle was gone.

Dark Glasses hoisted her up, dragging her toward the man with the knife. "You're him. The one on the roof. You had a rifle. I saw your face when you got in the SUV."

If he had a reaction, she couldn't see it through the mask of Kronos.

He came forward and grabbed her arm. She reached for his mask, but his knife slashed across her hand. The sharp pain stunned her long enough for him to drag her closer. He raised the blade again. Her eyes widened as fear gripped her heart, and she closed her eyes.

"Let her go!" Nate's voice. She opened her eyes as hope blossomed inside her.

NATE'S HEART HAMMERED in his ears. Mel was bleeding, but from this distance, he couldn't tell where she was injured. All the verbal wounds from the park were erased. All that mattered right now was getting her out alive.

The second man in the dark suit and glasses ran past him and out of the building, but Nate didn't move. He couldn't aim his Glock at them both, and he had to stay on the one with the hostage. The man in the Kronos mask pressed a blade to her throat until Mel squeaked. The sound gutted him, but Nate kept his sights lined up on the bastard's forehead.

Time slowed as Nate's finger caressed the trigger. His voice was as level as his aim. "Put down your weapon and let her go."

"For the Titans!" He buried his blade in Mel's chest

as Nate pulled the trigger.

Mel and the masked man crumpled to the ground. Nate sprinted forward, holstering his gun on the way. He fell to his knees, moving Mel away from the now-dead man. The golden mask was still on, but it had a new hole in the forehead that cracked down to the chin like a sick Greek version of the Phantom of the Opera.

He kissed Mel's hair, eyeing the knife. Only the handle protruded from her chest, the blade buried deep in the left side. She winced. "It hurts. Get it out."

She was bleeding but not hemorrhaging. "You need a hospital," he said softly to her, trying to keep her calm. "If it nicked your heart or an artery, you could bleed out if I remove it. Stay with me."

He pulled out his phone with one hand, holding Mel in his other. "Yeah, it's Detective Malone. Get the paramedics here. Now. Stab wound." He gave them the cross streets and stroked her hair back from her face. "Hang on, baby. You've got to stay awake. They're on their way."

Her eyes fluttered open. "What I said… Not true… Didn't mean it."

"We can talk later. Save your strength."

"Maggie?"

He watched the door for any sign of the man in black returning. "She's safe. John's with her at the park."

"Good…" Her eyes drifted closed. Shit.

He tapped her cheek. "Mel? Open your eyes. Wake

up."

Sirens blared in the distance.

Come on...

He kissed her temple and whispered, "I'm not giving you up. Please, Mel. I love you."

The door burst open and in rushed two paramedics with a gurney. "We've got it from here."

He forced himself to turn her over to them. They slid her onto a crash board and took her vitals. Pulse was tacky, breathing shallow.

Nate gave them room to work, staying close enough to notice she didn't open her eyes again, even when they inspected where she'd been stabbed. He ground his teeth. Once they had her lifted onto the rolling gurney, the police pulled up. Nate rushed through his explanation about the dead assailant and let them know they could call him at the hospital.

MAGGIE RAN ACROSS the waiting room and flung her arms around his neck. He'd never been more grateful to see her. He closed his eyes, holding her tight.

John walked over and took the chair next to him. "Maggie insisted we come see you before I took her back to Mrs. Gaines."

She sat on his lap and patted over his heart. "Is Mel..." Her voice trembled. "Will she be okay?"

"I think so." He nodded, hoping he looked more

certain than he felt. "The doctors are fixing her up."

John met his eyes over her head. "They ID'ed the guy in the mask. Ben Rodgers."

"Does he work for Belkin Oil?"

"He's not on the employee roster, but we're running a background check now." John glanced at Maggie. "I should probably get her home. School in the morning."

Maggie lifted her head to look at Nate. "Can I stay with you? Please?"

Nate sighed. "It might be a long time before they finish with Mel. You should go home and sleep. I'll come by and see you tomorrow, okay?"

She slid off his lap. "Okay."

John squeezed his shoulder. "Keep me posted."

"Will do. Thanks for taking care of Maggie."

John nodded and they left him alone, the silence of the waiting room weighing on him. He fought to keep his eyes off the second hand on the wall clock. Mel had been in surgery for almost four hours now. He leaned back, rubbing his hands down his face.

If only he'd been faster, or shot first, or never walked away at the park, or done anything to avoid this outcome.

Before he could make himself insane, a doctor came through the door. "Are you Melanie Jacoby's husband?"

A small lie. It was the only way he could get to see her after surgery.

"Yeah." He stood, every muscle tense. "Is she all right?"

The doctor's single nod stole the breath from Nate's lungs.

"We repaired the damage. Thankfully the blade missed her heart and didn't puncture her lung. She and the baby should be fine. She's in recovery now. A nurse will come get you when she's conscious and stable."

Nate's pulse jumped a beat. "Excuse me? What?"

The doctor frowned. "She's in recovery. It shouldn't be long before you can see her."

"No." Nate fumbled for the words. "Before that. I thought you said…"

"Oh… You didn't know." The doctor's eyes widened, then he shook his head. "I'm sorry to spill the beans."

"So Melanie…Mel…she's…"

"Pregnant. Yes, the blood test was positive. She should definitely visit her doctor to get a due date and prenatal care soon." He held out his hand. "Congratulations."

Nate stared at his hand for a second. Maybe he'd drifted off in the waiting room. A baby? Mel had seemed so sure she was in the clear.

He gripped the doctor's hand. "Thanks for saving her."

"She's a fighter." The doctor smiled. "I just plugged the holes."

CHAPTER 19

"BEN IS DEAD." Ted stared at the back of his father's head. Although Ted had taken over Belkin Oil as CEO, his father was still chairman of the board and he wore the power like a king's robe.

Belkin, Sr. turned his chair around slowly. His gray eyes pinning his son where he stood. "You're sure his body won't lead the police to us?"

"No, he's not on the company payroll."

His father shook his head. "Damned waste. He was the first of the Order to take the bull by the horns and get rid of a muse."

"He won't be the last. I'm already grooming a new enforcer. A *better* enforcer. He follows orders."

Belkin, Sr. leaned back, his executive chair squealing in protest. "Good thinking. Does he know about the Order yet?"

Ted crossed his arms. "Not exactly. He thinks he does."

"Good." His father nodded. "Reconditioning is more successful the less he knows."

"You'll like him. Bryce isn't as...*driven* as Ben, but he'll do what he's told."

"No 'loose ends'?"

"Exactly." Ted dropped his arms to his sides, relaxing slightly. His father was taking the news much better than he had anticipated.

"Tie Ben to the C-4 so we're out of the police investigation. And have our investigator check into Bryce's background. Be sure he has no family to start missing him. If he's clear, bring him to me next week."

"I already did. He's estranged from his mother and he doesn't know his father."

His father actually smiled. "Good work."

Ted nodded and went to the door before his father could see how much his praise meant to him. Stopping at the door, Ted turned back. "Melanie Jacoby made it through surgery, by the way."

"As long as that detective is protecting her, she's not worth the risk." His father picked up a pen and began signing documents. "There are seven other muses. Perhaps one of them will be easier prey for our new enforcer."

The corners of Ted's mouth curved into a thoughtful smile. "I was thinking the same thing."

NATE FLINCHED WHEN the nurse called his name. He'd been lost in his jumbled thoughts, staring out the window as if something out there might tell him what to do next.

"I can take you to see Melanie."

"Thank you." He followed her, his heart racing.

Walking the white halls, he struggled to figure out what to say, what to do. And what would she want?

His own desires shocked him to his core. Never in his life had he ever considered having children. Besides having no inclination to get married, his only example of a father was a piece of shit. What if he became the same man?

But since Maggie came into his life, she'd wormed her way into his broken heart, and from the core of his being, he knew there was no way on earth he'd ever hurt her the way his father had scarred him.

He and the nurse turned the corner and entered the room. Mel was pale, but her weak smile brought unexpected tears to his eyes.

"I'll leave you two alone," said the nurse before vanishing down the hall.

Nate approached Mel's bedside. His stomach was tied in knots as he took her hand. "The doctor says you're going to be fine."

Mel squeezed his hand. "Yeah... Remind me never to get stabbed again."

A smile tugged at his lips as he bent to kiss her forehead. "I'm good with that plan."

"I must've been out awhile. I woke up married." Her eyes sparkled.

"Hope you don't mind." He chuckled and shook his head slowly. "It was the only way they'd let me in here with you." He met her eyes. "The doctor said you're a fighter."

She caressed his cheek. "I had unfinished business." Her smile faded. "I didn't mean what I said at the park. He was on the phone listening. I was trying to get you to take Maggie home—out of rifle range."

"I know."

She raised a brow. "You didn't look like you knew."

"Well I didn't right away." At the time, he'd been more pissed at himself for letting his guard down. Her words had only hurt because he'd let her into his heart. He cleared the lump of emotion from his throat. "But I figured it out." He sobered. "My instinct was to back off and shut you out of my life, but even before my birthmark started to burn, something occurred to me." He swallowed, forced himself to speak. "What you said didn't make sense…because I make you happy. We're good together."

His voice dropped to a raspy whisper. "And I'm *not* nothing. I never was. You were the one who made me believe that."

She wiped a tear from her cheek and lifted their joined hands to her lips. "I love you. I had to go with them to protect Maggie, but I *knew* you'd come for me, even though I told you not to."

"That's pretty 'glass half-full' for you, isn't it?"

"Yeah." Her face brightened a little. "You have that effect on me." She glanced down at her gown and back up at him. "I need to tell you something else, but you have to promise to remember that this has nothing to do with my having a near-death experience."

"Okay." He tensed but didn't retreat. Whatever she had to say, he could take it.

"When they gave me a choice, my life or Maggie's…" She shook her head. "I knew right then that… It's horrible timing, but…" She met his eyes. "I love that little girl, and I'd like to adopt her."

"No," Nate blurted without hesitation.

She frowned, shocked. He was the one who'd told her about the couple who had decided not to make Maggie part of their family. He'd said he wanted her to have a home; apparently just not one with Mel.

"Wait, that came out wrong." He pulled up a chair and sat beside her, fidgeting.

Nate Malone was fidgeting?

Maybe she was more lightheaded than she realized. "What's going on?"

He lifted his gaze, his expression unreadable. "I need to tell you something, a few things, but they might be a little out of order."

She winced a little. This couldn't be good. She rolled her eyes. "Well the setup sounds great so far."

"Sorry." He chuckled, but the uncertainty still lined his eyes. "The thing is, none of this has to do with the attack, and I don't want you to think it does, so I'm not sure if I should wait…"

She laced her fingers with his. "We've been through hell and back the past few weeks. As long as it doesn't involve you leaving, I can handle it."

"Okay." He kissed her forehead and stared into her eyes. "Until the Kronos guys crashed the party, being at the park with you and Maggie, going to her class…" He shook his head slowly. "I didn't want it to end. I *don't* want it to end."

He searched her face. For what, she couldn't be sure. She worried her lower lip to keep from speaking.

Nate pressed his mouth to her knuckles and met her eyes. "I don't want you to adopt her…" He swallowed. "I want *us* to adopt her."

"Us?" Mel's heart pounded, her eyes brimming with tears. Nate paled at her response, and she squeezed his hand. "Yes. I'm just… I'm shocked."

He nodded with a tentative smile. "See what I mean about it all being out of order? I should be asking you to marry me first."

She laughed. "According to the hospital, we're already married."

Nate didn't laugh or smile. His eyes never left hers. "I will do my best to fill your glass when it starts to get half-empty, keep you and our family safe, and love you for the rest of my life." His voice trembled. "Melanie Jacoby, will you marry me?"

Tears slipped down her cheeks as she smiled. "Yes," she whispered. "Yes." She leaned up to hug him and winced, setting off an IV alarm behind her. Settling back on the pillow, she chuckled. "I wish I weren't lying in a hospital gown and we could celebrate, but come to think of it…" She gestured to the lifesaving equipment. "It's probably perfect for me and my muse."

Then a tear escaped from the corner of Nate's eye, too. "I have one more bomb to drop. I wish it could wait, but I don't want you to hear it from anyone else while you're here in the hospital."

She frowned. "You didn't get in trouble for shooting that bastard, did you?"

"No. At least not yet." He wiped his cheek and leaned in closer. "But what I'm about to tell you has nothing to do with my proposal, all right? Telling the hospital you were my wife came out of my mouth as naturally as telling criminals they have the right to an attorney. No one was more surprised than I was to realize I wanted to get married, but being with you is where I always want to be."

"Okay." Her pulse bounced on the monitor. Did they find cancer in her chest while they were sewing her up?

Nate rested his large hand on her abdomen. "Maggie is going to be a big sister."

Mel paused for a second while her muse caught up. She wasn't dying. The puzzle piece fell into place.

She brought her hand down to cover his and let out a soft gasp. "We're having a baby?"

Nate nodded. "The doctor thought we already knew."

Mel choked on a happy sob, squeezing his hand. "And you swear you're not proposing out of obligation, right?"

"I swear." He smiled, and her belly warmed. "I want to marry you because you make my life crazy in the best kind of way. I want to see you every day and raise our family together."

She grinned, overwhelmed on all fronts. "I need to tell my sisters." Her gaze snapped to his face. "And you need to tell John. He's going to think the world ended."

"Nah, he'll cover and say something like 'I knew you'd come around someday, Malone.'"

John was a good guy in spite of their rocky first meeting.

Mel smiled up at Nate. "Callie's going to blow a gasket."

He chuckled. "She better be happy, or she and I will be having some words."

"You're so sexy when you go all Guardian like that."

Nate laughed and leaned down to hold her tight. "Heal up." He kissed her lips, slow and tender, until her toes curled. "I need to let Maggie know you're all right."

Mel grinned. "Don't tell her about us yet. I want to be there."

"You got it."

CHAPTER 20

WITH THE HELP of Mel's sisters, Nate got all of her things packed up and moved to his place before she returned from the hospital. They peppered him with questions, but he managed to keep quiet about the engagement, letting them know they had decided to keep living together even though the danger was over for now.

He left the boxes labeled and neatly stacked in the corner of his dining area so she could put her stuff away wherever she wanted. His days in the bachelor pad were numbered. And he was surprised to realize he didn't give a shit. Being with her made his old life seem so…empty. He wasn't going to miss it.

During her hospital stay, they'd made plans for their future. As soon as she was up to it, they'd start looking at new places with three bedrooms, one for Maggie and one for Baby Malone. Mel came up with the nickname, and his heart swelled every time he thought of it. As a kid, "family" meant pain and fear, but with Mel, he found himself eager to make new memories.

She showed him a whole different world, one full of

strength, loyalty, and laughter.

He was a lucky bastard. And any time those old feelings of panic and insecurity crept up on him, he was quick to remind himself of that fact.

It also kept his mind off the debriefing at work. He was cleared for duty after shooting the suspect, but the relief didn't come as he'd expected. There was still a lingering foreboding in his gut. The guy in dark glasses had gotten away.

Nate had given the sketch artist his best description, but all his attention had been on Mel at the time. He didn't get a good look at the man. And so far, they hadn't gotten any hits on the composite. The man in the mask wasn't working alone, though, and it was more than likely that there were more men in golden Kronos masks out there.

He wanted to believe it was over with one bullet, but his instincts told him not to drop his guard.

John crossed his arms, trying not to smile. "Don't you have someplace to go, Malone?"

He glanced up at his partner with a grin. "Yeah, I'm heading out now."

Mel was coming home today. To say he'd been counting down the minutes would've been an understatement. He set the composite of the man in sunglasses aside and grabbed his jacket. "Catch you later."

John nodded. "Homecoming party still on for tomorrow?"

"Yeah. My place at five. Callie will be there to let you in."

Nate made the drive to the hospital in record time. When he got to Mel's room, she was already up and dressed. He shook his head. "Damn, you're beautiful."

She smiled and walked straight into his arms. He embraced her, careful not to hold her too tightly.

Her lips brushed his neck. "I'm not going to break."

"I'm not taking any chances."

She pulled back, her smile warming him all over. "As long as you're not planning to poke my wound, I'm all right. Really." She rose up on her toes and brushed her lips against his. "See?"

"Good to know." He grinned, stealing one more kiss.

He carried her bag in one hand and held her hand with the other. He helped her into the car and happily left the medical center in the rearview mirror.

"Are you hungry?" he asked.

She shook her head. "Not really. Just anxious to get home."

He rested his hand on her thigh. "Then home it is."

"And you didn't tell anyone?"

He chuckled. "No one would believe we were getting married and having a baby even if I told them." He squeezed her leg. "But when I make a promise, I keep it."

"Sorry. Tough to shut down the muse sometimes."

"I did start the paperwork to adopt Maggie, but I haven't said anything to her yet and I swore Mr. and Mrs. Gaines to secrecy." He glanced at her and back to the road. "She made me crazy trying to get me to take her to the hospital to visit you."

"Sorry they wouldn't let her in."

He hadn't told Maggie the hospital denied her. Family members only. He'd opted for telling her only grownups could visit. "Pretty soon we'll all be family and it won't be a problem again."

"Thanks for waiting so we can talk to her together."

He parked the car at his place and took her hand again. "I'm new to this whole relationship thing, but as I understand it, we're a team, right?"

She nodded and got out of the car.

Once he had her and her things inside, she walked toward the bedroom. "I need a shower."

He tensed up, imagining her fainting and hitting her head. Maybe her muse was rubbing off on him.

As if she could read his mind, she glanced back. "I might also need a shower buddy, just in case I get lightheaded."

A smile tugged at his lips. "Safety first, right?"

MEL UNBUTTONED HER shirt, eyeing Nate's muscular

back as he bent to turn on the hot water. Her wound was still bruised and tender, but she was desperate to be close to him, skin to skin. Since the attack, sleeping alone had been a challenge. Her dreams were haunted by that damn mask of Kronos' face.

Nate straightened up and closed the lid on the toilet. He took a seat and stared up at her. "I can wait here…"

She shook her head, working her lower lip with her teeth. "I need you close."

He didn't question her. Without a word, he tugged off his T-shirt and tossed it on the floor. Seeing his toned chest, his abs like iron, stoked her hunger for him, leaving no room for fear. This was her Guardian. *Hers.*

For the first time since she woke up in the hospital, she felt safe.

With the buttons of her top undone, she started to slide it off and winced.

Nate was on his feet right behind her. "Let me help."

He slid the shirt down her arms and came around in front of her. His gaze wandered to her stitches. "I'm so sorry I didn't get there sooner."

"He'll never touch me again. That's all that matters."

His eyes met hers. "Never again."

"Every time I see this scar, I'm not going to remember him. I'm going to remember this was the day you saved my life."

He closed the distance between them, kissing her lips, hungry but still tender. She ran her hands down his chest, enjoying the way his muscles contracted at her touch. Without breaking the kiss, she unbuttoned his pants and lowered the zipper.

He caught her hand. "Are you sure? I don't want to hurt you."

"We'll be careful." Her heart pounded, heat smoldering low in her belly. "I need you. Please."

She hadn't told Nate about the nightmares or how she'd endured her hospital stay by imagining being naked in his strong arms. It was their future together that inspired her healing, and she didn't want to let the crazy man in the gold mask steal any more of their time. They were alive and in love. Fear could take a flying leap.

He searched her eyes and finally kissed her slowly. He rested his forehead against hers. "I need you, too."

She tried to slide his pants down, but Nate came to the rescue, getting his jeans off and then helping her with her sweatpants. He tested the water in the shower and then took her hand as she stepped inside.

The warm water shocked her system. She trembled, and Nate turned them both so the spray hit his back instead of hers, still protecting her. "Is it too hot?'

"No." A smile curved on her lips. "It's just been awhile since I felt warm and safe. I forgot how good it feels."

His shoulders relaxed and he bent forward, his lips caressing her shoulder as he turned slowly. The warm water didn't surprise her this time. Nate lathered shampoo into her hair, his fingers massaging her scalp until she moaned. One hand drifted down her back, cupping her backside and pressing her closer to him. She opened her eyes to find him staring at her face.

His voice was deep, filled with emotion. "I love you."

She reached up to caress his cheek. "I love you, too."

He bent his knees, sliding his hands down her back to grip her hips. She wrapped her legs around his waist, careful not to bump her stitches.

"Are you all right?" he asked. "Did I hurt you?"

"I'm fine." She leaned in closer and whispered against his ear, "I bet you've never had sex with a fiancée before."

"It's my first time." The corner of his mouth quirked up into a sexy crooked smile as he slowly entered her, careful to hold her steady. His teeth teased her ear. "Be gentle with me."

Mel tipped her head back into the water, moaning and laughing all at once. She held tight as he rocked slowly into her, grinding to keep from jostling her. The pleasure, the connection; they were healing her. "I missed this."

"I missed you, too." He kissed his way down to her neck as he turned to rest her back against the wall of the shower. He lifted his head. "Too cold?"

"No." She shook her head. "Don't stop."

He slid a hand between them, stroking her in time with his thrusts as his lips claimed hers. She moaned into the kiss, working her hips into him until they both surrendered. Her nails dug into his shoulder as they crashed over the edge together.

Nate straightened after a minute, water dripping from his hair. "I need to put you down before we fall."

Mel let her legs slide down from his waist as he lowered her. Even after her feet were on the floor, he kept one arm around her, steadying her. She definitely got lucky the day the gods chose Nate as her Guardian.

"Nate, can you tack this side of the banner up?" Callie held the other end up from the top of the stepladder.

He pushed a pin through the Welcome home! banner and into the ceiling. On the other side of the room, Trinity and Polly blew up balloons with Maggie. None of them knew about the engagement, the baby, or the adoption paperwork he and Mel had already started.

They wanted to share the news together to all their loved ones at once.

And she had no idea about the party. Mel's parents came into town after he told them about the attack, and they were distracting her today so he and her sisters could decorate.

So while the muses were plotting to surprise Mel, they had their own surprise coming…

John came in the door with his wife, Beth, and Nate introduced her to Mel's sisters.

Nate shook John's hand and kissed Beth's cheek. "I'll be back soon." He turned toward Maggie. "Ready to pick up Mel?"

Maggie bounced to her feet. "Yes! But I won't tell her about the party."

He held out his hand and she took it, waving at the others. "See you soon."

THE PLAN WAS to grab Mel from the hotel where her folks were staying. It would give them time to sneak over to Nate's place with the others and also give Mel and him a private moment to talk to Maggie.

The second they entered the hotel lobby, Maggie made a break for it, running to hug Mel. "I was scared."

Mel smiled at Nate from over Maggie's curls. "I'm all right." She pulled back, holding Maggie out at an arm's length. "So what'd I miss?"

That was all it took. Maggie rambled on about school, her new friends, and her teacher, while Nate said his good-byes to her parents. He turned toward Mel and smiled. He loved seeing her with Maggie. He hoped the feeling wouldn't ever wear off. He never wanted to take his new family for granted.

Once he had them both in the car, he glanced at Mel and she squeezed his thigh. He winked and pulled out of the parking lot. Instead of heading back to his place, though, he drove to his spot at the beach.

Maggie got out of the car and frowned. "This isn't where we're a-post to be, Uncle Nate."

He caught Mel's hand, his fingers twining with hers. "We came here first so we could talk to you before we went back to my house."

She glanced between the two of them and finally nodded. "Okay."

Nate herded her over to the bench. It seemed like ages since he had sat in this spot and first shown Mel his birthmark, when she'd told him the truth about their connection.

Maggie was between them now, swinging her feet that didn't quite reach the ground.

Nate patted her leg. "We wanted you to know our surprise before anyone else."

Her eyes widened. "A surprise?"

Nate nodded slowly, his eyes meeting Mel's. "I asked Mel to marry me."

Maggie's jaw dropped.

Mel grinned. "And I said yes."

Maggie put a small hand on each of their knees, her gap-toothed grin at full power. "You're getting married?"

"Yes." Mel placed her hand over Maggie's. "And if

you're okay with it, we want you to come live with us."

Nate held his breath. Maggie spun toward him, her bright eyes brimming with tears. "You mean it?"

Nate nodded, his own eyes burning. "I'd like to be your dad if you'll have me."

Maggie lurched forward, her arms clamping around his neck and her little sobs breaking his heart. He held her close while Mel embraced them both. He didn't know how long they sat like that, clinging to one another, but Maggie finally whispered, "I love you."

He laughed, choking on a tight throat. "I love you, too, Maggie."

Mel pulled back a little, her voice soft. "We have one more surprise."

Maggie loosened her hold on Nate and turned toward Mel, her breath still hitching. "Another one?"

Mel nodded slowly and met his eyes. Nate wanted to memorize every second of this moment. The way the sea breeze pulled at Mel's hair, the way her skin glowed, the way she looked at him and told him she loved him without saying a word.

Her gaze moved to Maggie as she took her hand. "You're going to be a big sister."

A wrinkle formed in the middle of Maggie's forehead for a second, and then it gave way to a joyful smile. She hopped off the bench, facing both of them. "You're having a baby, too?"

"Yes." Mel paused. "And it would be the luckiest baby on earth if it got to have you for a big sister."

Maggie took each of their hands and squeezed them tight. "This is the best day ever!"

Nate couldn't contain his joy any longer. He shot out from the bench and caught Maggie around the waist, lifting her into the air. He spun her in a circle, drinking in her laughter before hugging her again, his eyes on Mel over at the bench.

"I agree, kid. Days don't get much better than this one."

Mel held Maggie's hand as they walked across the parking lot toward Nate's condo. Half of her still struggled to believe that today was real. She was going to marry the most amazing man she'd ever met, become a mother to a feisty seven-year-old, and in a few more months, she'd have two children.

Her head was spinning, but as much as her mind fought to work through all the new changes coming her way, her heart was overflowing with joy. There were so many more blessings in her life than she ever dreamed she'd have.

Nate opened the door to his place then, and a roomful of her favorite people shouted, "Welcome home, Mel!"

Her heart nearly burst. "Aw, thanks, you guys…"

The second the door closed behind them, Maggie squealed, "They're getting married, and we're going to be a family!"

Mel laughed while Nate mussed Maggie's curls.

John made his way through all her sisters and stood in front of her, his expression blank. "I told you, Nate doesn't do relationships."

Mel wasn't sure how to respond, but before it got too awkward, John grinned and opened his arms. "Glad you showed him the light."

Mel accepted his hug, and John whispered against her ear, "Take good care of my partner."

She nodded as she pulled back. "I will." Then she noticed her parents lurking over in the kitchen area. "You were in on this, too?"

Her mom had a sheepish grin on her face. "It was Nate's idea."

Before Mel could reply, Callie came up to her with a hand on her hip, a smile threatening to break through her mock anger. "We had a pact, remember?"

Nate stiffened, but Mel shook her head. "I love you, Callie, and I hope the fates put a man in your path that makes you kiss our pact good-bye, too."

"Don't wish that on me." Callie chuckled and came forward to hug her. "We still have a theater to restore."

Mel squeezed her tight and stepped back. "I know. And we'll have even more hands to fix it now."

Nate slid his arm around her waist. "Maggie and I will help." His green eyes met hers, making her tingle all over.

Mel pulled her gaze back to her sisters. "And one

more thing…" She ran her fingers through the back of Maggie's curls. "You want to tell them?"

Maggie nodded with a grin. "I'm going to be a big sister."

Mel's sisters surrounded her while Nate stood beside John. He smiled at her and mouthed, *I love you.*

Her eyes brimmed with happy tears. The muse was silent inside her. Today, her glass wasn't half-empty.

It was overflowing.

Thanks for reading! If you enjoyed the book, please consider posting a review. It really helps other readers discover the series too.

The concept for The Muse Chronicles was inspired by a short story I wrote while I was taking up Ray Bradbury's Challenge to write 52 Stories in 52 weeks. *Unemployed Muses Anonymous* is part of the *Forgotten Treasures* anthology.

I'm so excited to finally be able to bring the series to life!

I give away free short stories with my monthly newsletter, along with eBooks and updates about new releases and sales.

You can sign up for my newsletter here: goo.gl/qaIIiS

Other Novels by Lisa Kessler

The Muse Chronicles
LURE OF OBSESSION
LEGEND OF LOVE

The Night Series
NIGHT WALKER
NIGHT THIEF
NIGHT DEMON
NIGHT ANGEL
NIGHT CHILD

The Moon Series
MOONLIGHT
HUNTER'S MOON
BLOOD MOON
HARVEST MOON
ICE MOON
BLUE MOON

Stand Alone Works
BEG ME TO SLAY
FORGOTTEN TREASURES
ACROSS THE VEIL

Acknowledgments

When the idea for the Muse Chronicles came to me, it was my amazing agent, Laurie McLean, who first encouraged me to self-publish this series. Then my grandmother helped me to make it a reality. Thanks for your support for this new venture!

Self-publishing is a big project that I couldn't do alone, so first off, thanks to Danielle Poiesz from Double Vision Editorial. It's so great to work with you again! And a big thank-you to Fiona Jayde for taking my vision for the Muse Chronicles and making such a gorgeous logo and cover. You rock! Thanks to my intrepid beta readers, who also helped me on the back cover copy. Denise Fluhr, Heather Cox, and Elizabeth Neal, you guys are the BEST!

Big thanks to the Night Angel Legion for all your support! It's scary to dip my toe into indie publishing, but you all have my back and I love you for it!

I also need to give a shout out to Eleanor Nystrom and the RWASD Sprinters for inspiring me when I was in the homestretch, writing this book until all hours of the night. You guys made it fun!

Big thanks to Arianne Cruz for proofreading for me, and Guillian and the team at Inscribe for helping me get the word out about the new series!

And finally, thanks to my family and my husband, Ken, for all your support. I couldn't do this without you!

Lisa Kessler is an Amazon Best Selling author of dark paranormal fiction. She's a two-time San Diego Book Award winner for Best Published Fantasy-Sci-fi-Horror and Best Published Romance, an Award of Excellence for Best Paranormal Romance, as well as the Romance Through the Ages Award for Best Paranormal and Best First Book.

Her short stories have been published in print anthologies and magazines, and her vampire story, Immortal Beloved, was a finalist for a Bram Stoker award.

When she's not writing, Lisa is a professional vocalist, and has performed with San Diego Opera as well as other musical theater companies in San Diego.

You can learn more at Lisa-Kessler.com

Printed in Great Britain
by Amazon